A Viking

for the

ISCOUNTESS

MICHELLE
WILLINGHAM

A MOST PECULIAR SEASON

Published by Michelle Willingham
www.michellewillingham.com

ISBN-13: 978-0-9906345-1-5

Cover by Robert Papp and The Font Diva
Interior Formatting by Author E.M.S.

Published in the United States of America.

To Linda—

Enjoy my Viking!

Michelle
Willi...

OTHER BOOKS BY
MICHELLE WILLINGHAM

Forbidden Viking Series
(Viking Age Ireland)

To Sin with a Viking
To Tempt a Viking

A Most Peculiar Season Series
(Regency)

A Viking for the Viscountess
A Maiden for the Marquess (coming in 2015)

Secrets in Silk Series
(Regency Scotland)

Undone by the Duke
Unraveled by the Rebel
Undressed by the Earl
Unlaced by the Outlaw

MacEgan Brothers Series
(Medieval Ireland)

Her Warrior Slave
"The Viking's Forbidden Love-Slave" (novella)
Her Warrior King
Her Irish Warrior
The Warrior's Touch
Taming Her Irish Warrior
"The Warrior's Forbidden Virgin" (novella)
"Voyage of an Irish Warrior" (novella)

Surrender to an Irish Warrior
"Pleasured by the Viking" (novella)
"Lionheart's Bride" (novella)
Warriors in Winter

The MacKinloch Clan Series
(Medieval Scotland)

Claimed by the Highland Warrior
Seduced by Her Highland Warrior
"Craving the Highlander's Touch" (novella)
Tempted by the Highland Warrior
"Rescued by the Highland Warrior" (novella in the
Highlanders anthology)

The Accidental Series
(Victorian England/Fictional Province of Lohenberg)

"An Accidental Seduction" (novella)
The Accidental Countess
The Accidental Princess
The Accidental Prince

Other Titles

"Innocent in the Harem"
(A novella of the sixteenth-century Ottoman Empire)
"A Wish to Build a Dream On"
(time travel novella to medieval Ireland)

CHAPTER ONE

H e would die in an hour. Perhaps sooner, if the gods called to him.

Arik Thorgrim lay prone upon the deck of his ship, feeling his strength slipping away as the blood pooled beneath him. The battle-ax wound was too deep, and he'd already seen the grim looks upon the faces of his men. They knew, as he did, that his life was over and he would soon join his brother warriors in Valhalla.

The chill of the night air turned his skin cold, numbing him to the brutal pain. Though most men might fear death, he welcomed it. For this night he would claim immortality and leave behind the woman who had betrayed him.

He closed his eyes, trying to blot out the image of Svala's face. Her long golden hair had flowed against her hips, her beauty tantalizing the dreams of any man. A smile from her was beyond price, worth every last piece of gold he possessed.

And then, as if to taunt him, he recalled her bare legs

1

wrapped around Eyker's waist, her head thrown back in mindless lust. Arik had stumbled upon them together when he'd returned to their camp after raiding the southern coast. He had believed Svala was a shy virgin, only to learn that she'd given herself to his enemy.

Her infidelity and lies had sliced deeper than any blade. But when he'd gone to murder Eyker, the man's brother had struck him in the back with a battle-ax.

So be it. There was a place in the frost-laden depths of *Hel* for a coward without honor.

The waves of the sea grew rougher, and dimly, he heard the call of his *böndr* as the ship tossed. The men had sailed with him over the past few months, leaving behind their families and farms to seek wealth. His brother, Magnus, had built a settlement along the northeast coast of East Anglia, and Arik had asked his men to bring him there. He could not survive the journey to Rogaland to see his parents again—but he could reach his brother's home within hours.

Magnus was his closest sibling, and if the gods willed it, he might look upon his brother's face before he died. He wanted his body to be buried with honor.

Arik lay motionless, letting the sea take him. The ship rolled him to his back, and the searing pain nearly sent him into a void of darkness. He stared up at the clouded moon, while it transformed into an orange haze of blood. A dark shadow eclipsed the surface, and his vision wavered.

Would that I could have another chance at life.

The icy hand of Death beckoned closer, and he felt his body trembling with the last fight to live. Regrets flowed over him, but there was nothing that would change his fate.

He'd have made far different choices. He wouldn't

have left his father in reckless defiance to go a-viking. He would have taken a quiet woman as his wife. Then at least he'd have a son or daughter of his blood to live on. But now, only his brother remained.

When he blinked, there were no other clouds in the sky, and the night was clear. Strange for it to be so, while violent sea waves tossed his wooden vessel. He thought he spied another ship, a strange wooden boat that did not resemble anything he'd ever seen before. The mast towered over the deck, and he could only imagine how large the sails would be when they were unfurled. These men, too, were caught in the storm.

Although the ship lurched, Arik's wounded body remained motionless, as if an invisible hand pinned him to the deck. The swells crashed against the side of the boat, and he feared it was Jörmungand, the serpent of Midgard, rising from the depths to devour them all. Amid the roar of the sea, he heard the shouts of terror from his men before they were swept under by the frigid waves, their lives claimed as sacrifice.

Silence cloaked the night, and the agony of his wound began to fade. Arik took a breath and saw that the blood upon his hands was gone. When he reached back to touch the ragged skin where the battle-ax had cut him down, he found that it had healed completely. A coldness drifted over his skin, but he refused to let the fear gain a foothold.

He was dead now. There was no other explanation for his wound disappearing. No doubt his body now rested on the bottom of the sea. He had to finish this journey to the afterworld alone, and he suspected he would soon see the spirits of those who had fallen before him.

Not yet, he heard a woman's voice whisper upon the wind.

He blinked, wondering if he had only imagined the words. All was still now, and the sea had calmed. Arik rose to his feet, testing his strength to stand. At the front of the boat, he stared into the darkness, hoping for a glimpse of Asgard, where the gods dwelled. If there was land nearby, he couldn't see it. He leaned back to look at the stars, trying to determine his whereabouts. The waves bobbed his ship, but the motion was gentle. With his hand upon the rudder, he questioned whether to steer or let the sea guide him. In the end, he surrendered command of the vessel, for he had no way of knowing where the gods would lead him.

As the sea shifted and blurred all around him, he suddenly spied the prone figure of a body in the water. Her golden hair streamed around her, and his heart seized up, not knowing if it was Svala. Had she joined him in death? Or had the gods sent her to him, as a gift?

Whether or not she was real, Arik didn't hesitate as he dove from the ship to save her.

NORFOLK, ENGLAND
ONE THOUSAND YEARS LATER

Juliana Arthur, the Viscountess Hawthorne, tucked her son into bed, kissing his forehead. "Sleep well, Harry." The boy smiled up at her and snuggled deeper into the threadbare sheets. She had dressed him in two nightshirts and woolen socks, as well as a cap to keep him warm. Often at night, he would slip out of his trundle bed and crawl inside her own bed, while the wind rattled the shutters of their small house.

"Will we go back to Hawthorne House in the morning?" he asked.

"We might, if your father returns." She smoothed his hair and gave an encouraging smile. "Now close your eyes."

As soon as he did, her smile faded. She had been telling Harry the lie for months now. They could not return to Hawthorne House, no matter how badly she wanted to. For the past six years it had been her sanctuary. She loved every blade of grass on the estate, and it had become her home after the viscount had abandoned her there.

Juliana supposed she ought to be devastated that her husband had gone traveling on the Continent without her. She did want William to come back—truly she did. But not because she loved him or because she missed him. No, she wanted him back to save them from this poverty.

God forgive her, she'd been so glad at first, when she'd heard the news that he might never return. She'd swept her infant son into her arms, hugging him with joy. No longer would William tell her how worthless she was, how fortunate she was to be with him. He wouldn't give her orders on how to dress, what ladylike pursuits to indulge in, or how she should best please him in bed. Her son would never know his father, and nothing could have dimmed her elation at that moment.

But then, a solicitor had arrived at Hawthorne House six months ago, informing her that her marriage was invalid and she'd been nothing more than William's mistress. Her husband's brother, Marcus, had swiftly stripped her son of his inheritance and title, and though she'd tried to fight back, he would not allow it.

"You were never his wife," Marcus said coldly. "His mistress, perhaps, but nothing more."

"But I was," she whispered. "We eloped in Scotland. I signed the registry."

"There was no registry. And no written record of the marriage." Marcus folded his hands, with not a trace of sympathy in his demeanor. "My brother deceived you into believing it, likely so you would share his bed." When she started to argue again, he cut her off. "You're a practical woman, Juliana. Why would a viscount wed a fisherman's daughter?"

He made it sound as if she was no better than a scullery maid. Yes, her father had been a common man, but her mother was nobility.

"My grandfather is a baron," she argued. "And William loved me."

"Whether or not he loved you is beside the point. You were never married, and your son is a bastard."

Her mouth moved to deny his words, but no sound came out. She clenched her knuckles hard, feeling as if she'd entered a nightmare from which she couldn't wake up.

"Didn't you ever wonder why he hid you away in the country, never bringing you to London? It was because he didn't marry you at all."

Deep inside, she feared Marcus was right. She'd spent months paying runners to search for a record of their elopement. And still, the search had come up with nothing.

Either her husband had lied to her, or Marcus was lying to prevent her son from inheriting. He'd escorted them out of Hawthorne House with hardly more than a trunk of clothes. To keep Harry from being afraid, she'd told him that they were going to visit his grandfather. She'd woven an elaborate tale of how they would spend a few months by the sea and he could build castles in the sand.

Her life had felt like that sand castle, crumbling to pieces all around her. Especially when her father had died a few weeks later, leaving her grief-stricken.

Quiet descended over the house, and her maid, Grelod, drew her chair closer to the fire beside the sleeping dog. The older woman had been with her ever since Juliana had been a little girl and spoke only a little English. She had sought work in London, after leaving Norway, and had found a position when the housekeeper took pity on her. Grelod had been a favorite servant of the baroness, Juliana's grandmother, for she worked hard and said nothing.

Keeping her voice low, the old woman murmured in Norwegian, "It's not right, the two of you living in a place such as this. It's hardly fit for a beggar."

"I have nowhere else to go, and you know this."

"Your grandmother ought to have opened her doors to you." Grelod picked up the mending and muttered to herself, as she threaded her needle. "They might have cut off your mother after she wed your father, but that was no fault of yours."

"She did invite me to visit, but I would rather drown myself than accept help from her." Juliana moved her own stool beside the fire, watching the flames in the hearth. "Lady Traveston is a horrid woman."

"She did give you a Season," her maid pointed out.

"Only because it was my mother's last wish." And because her grandmother had wanted to mold her into a lady. Juliana had mistakenly thought that it would be a wonderful chance to meet a husband. She shuddered at the memory. The baroness had drilled months' worth of lessons and etiquette into her brain, as if she were preparing Juliana for war. And although she'd married a viscount, her grandmother had shown little satisfaction in the match. She'd never approved of William and had been aghast when they'd eloped.

A gust of wind blew through the crevices in the walls, and Juliana leaned over to bring the blanket up to Harry's neck. A bleakness caught at her heart. She had to do something to get her son out of this place. Soon, she would have no choice but to seek help from her grandparents. Lord Traveston might have abandoned his daughter and granddaughter, but she believed Lady Traveston would find a place for them to stay if Juliana groveled enough.

It was still a last resort.

Restlessness flowed within her veins as she paced across the cottage, worrying over how to find the evidence of her marriage. "Go out and have a walk," Grelod ordered. "You'll feel better for it."

"It's too dark," Juliana protested. "And I shouldn't leave Harry."

She started to walk toward the rocking chair, when Grelod caught her hand. "You're troubled, and the night air will do you good. Go, and you'll find the answers you've been seeking."

"The moonlight won't solve our problems, Grelod," she argued. "Only William can put everything to rights." If her husband returned, he could bring them back to Hawthorne House, admitting that their marriage had been valid.

"His ship might return," Grelod admitted. "Give an offering to the gods, and see what happens."

"An offering?" She hid a smile at the old woman's

superstitions. Grelod had always believed in magic and folklore. She had woven stories over the years at bedtime, legends that she was convinced were true, though Juliana now knew they had only been tales. Grelod's beliefs were a part of her, and she fervently upheld the old Norse traditions. At night, she often told Harry stories about the goddess Freya and her children of the moon. Though Juliana didn't believe in any of that, she saw no harm in indulging her maid.

"Give the gods a lock of your hair. Or a drop of your blood," the woman suggested. "Perhaps it will conjure up the help you need."

Juliana squeezed Grelod's hand, knowing her maid was only trying to help. She did want a chance to be alone, and strolling outside might clear her wayward thoughts. "I'll go for a walk. Watch over Harry and call out if he needs me."

Behind her, she heard the woman muttering incantations and words she didn't understand. Juliana sighed and reached for her cloak and bonnet.

The wind had stirred up, pulling the gray waves against the shore. She walked along the water's edge, while a full orange moon bathed the shore in a shimmer of gold. One could almost believe that a night like this could hold a bit of magic.

She drew her cloak around her, holding fast to her bonnet as the night air buffeted it. Ahead, she spied her father's boat, and a pang caught her heart. He'd been a fisherman all his life, and the battered wood seemed to draw her closer.

When she walked to the edge of the pier, she stepped inside the vessel, remembering the days when he'd taken her out to the sea, teaching her to fish. Being here, she could almost smell the familiar scent of tobacco. He'd been the most wonderful father, and she missed him dearly. Sometimes if she closed her eyes, she could remember the warmth of his embrace and his quiet love.

He'd been her steadfast rock, all her life—especially after her mother had died. A tightness clenched her gut as she stared up at the moon. *What am I supposed to do now, Father? How can I support my son, when I don't know if William is alive or dead?*

The wind shifted, filling up the mainsail. Juliana frowned, for she hadn't untied it. How had it come unfurled? It was almost as if an unseen presence had emerged.

Don't be silly. There is no such thing as a ghost. She pushed back the thought, trying to find a logical explanation. The sail had been tied up when she'd climbed aboard the boat, but somehow, it must have broken free. She fought with the canvas and ropes, trying to bring it back down again, but another gust of wind made her stumble. The sail swung out, the wooden boom cracking against her forehead.

The vicious pain made her cry out, and she knelt down in the boat, lowering her head to fight the dizziness. She'd never expected a storm to be brewing, not when the night had been so calm.

A moment later, the vessel started to float away from the dock, though she couldn't understand how. Without someone untying the ropes, there was no way it could break free of the moorings. But the wind strengthened, filling up the sail as if an invisible force were pulling her out into the open sea.

Juliana fumbled with the ropes, fighting to reverse her direction, but the wind was too strong. Even when she put her full weight against the sail, it didn't move. Panic sharpened within her as the boat sailed farther away from the dock.

No. She couldn't let this happen. She tore off her gloves, pulling with all her might. But even that wasn't enough to bring her back.

Her head ached, swelling up from the wound. Terror wrapped around her heart, for the boat was taking her too far away from the shore. And then how could she return to Harry? Though she didn't want to leave the safety of the boat, she saw no other choice but to swim back.

Steeling herself, Juliana slid both legs over the side of the boat, pushing herself into the frigid water. She strained with her feet to touch the bottom, but her head went underwater. What had happened? Now it seemed that the shore was twice as far away.

Impossible. She fought to swim back, though the weight of her clothes pulled her down. The waves sloshed against her face, and she began stripping away the layers, letting her cloak fall first. She tore off her bonnet and let it sink. The water was so cold, it froze her movements, making it harder to stay above the surface. As she struggled against the waves, the beach disappeared, leaving her alone on the sea.

Her heart was pounding with fear while her mind tried to make sense out of the impossible. Perhaps this was a dream and she was unconscious from the head injury. Dreams never made sense, and undoubtedly that was what this was.

The moon turned the color of blood, sliding back from behind a misty cloud. She tasted salt water, and her arms ached from swimming. But it did no good. The more she swam, the farther away land seemed.

It's not real, she told herself. *It can't be.*

The nightmare only worsened, and horror washed over

her when she saw that the boat was now gone. If she didn't get help soon, she was going to drown. She cried out, though it was hopeless to think that anyone would find her on a night like this.

Her arms grew heavy as she swam, her hair drenched against her face.

And when she saw the outline of another ship in the distance, she prayed to God that someone would save her.

Arik swam against the current, a rope tied to his waist. When he reached the woman, her hair obscured her face. He didn't know if the gods had brought Svala to him, in spite of his death. Had she somehow crossed over, losing her own life? Her body was so cold, he didn't know if she was alive or dead.

He pulled her into his arms, but she remained limp and motionless. He kicked hard to stay afloat as he swam back to his ship. It was a struggle to bring her on board, but he managed to get her to the deck. She coughed hard, her shoulders heaving. Tremors shook her body, and a strange gown clung to her. It was dull gray in color, but high-waisted, with a square neckline and a slender skirt.

The moon slid behind a cloud, shadowing her face. He couldn't tell if it was Svala or not, but they were the same height and form. Her long blond hair was unmistakable. If he was on his journey to the afterlife, surely this was his reward. Eyker's brother had offended the gods by striking a blow at his back, and Arik felt certain that Svala had been given to him as compensation.

She was cold, her body shivering violently from the icy water. He carried her to the back of the boat, away from the oars. Carefully, he stripped away her wet clothing, cutting the strange girdle that was tied tightly to her waist before removing his own garments. Body heat was the best way to warm both of them.

He laid her down upon a rough fur and covered her with his own flesh, cocooning her with another fur on top of himself. With her head tucked beneath his chin, he held her close, stroking her smooth skin.

Her hair smelled the same as he remembered, like crushed flowers and sweet herbs. He rested his face against her cheek, inhaling the sweetness of her. Desire roared through him, along with the pain of Svala's betrayal. She'd given herself to Eyker, sharing *his* bed instead of Arik's. She'd offered him words and promises, but never her body.

The grim rage festered within his mind, making Arik want to punish them both. He wanted to touch her, to bring her such raw need, she'd regret giving herself to another man. Her bare breasts rested against his chest, and the tight buds of her nipples aroused him. Odin's blood, she smelled good.

In his jealousy, he wanted to show her what she'd spurned, that he was a man who would pleasure her in a way she would never forget. He lowered his mouth to the curve of her throat, kissing her. Then he filled his palms with her breasts and set to work on seducing the woman he'd yearned for.

Juliana tried to open her eyes, but dizziness and darkness clung to her senses. Her skin was warm. So very warm. Against her body, she felt the heat of a man's skin.

Had William come back? Or was this a dream? She

thought about screaming, but his hands were stroking her bare back. It felt so good to be in safe, strong arms.

Yes, it was most definitely a dream. Ships didn't break free of knotted ropes, and land didn't disappear within seconds. She snuggled deeper into the man's arms and imagined that he was someone who adored her. Somehow she was safe within her own bed. The dreams of icy seawater and drowning were gone, and in their place was a fantasy she'd conjured in her mind.

The gentle touches moved from her spine to cup her breast. Against his palm, her nipples tightened, and she couldn't suppress the catch of her breath. The dream had become erotic, and she allowed her imagination to pull her into a deeper pleasure.

You will forget everything about him when I have finished with you, came the man's voice in a half-remembered language.

His words startled her. Was her dream man speaking of William? Juliana rather hoped so. She wanted to forget about her husband's demanding nature and the way he'd visited her bed, expecting her to scream his name or some other nonsense. What was there to scream about?

Her imagination settled back, enjoying the skilled hands that caressed her breasts, drawing out an echo of sensation between her legs. She had never felt this way before, with arousing liquid desires that raced through her skin. She reached out, not knowing what was happening to her, but her phantom lover bent to her throat, his mouth kissing her pulse point while his hands threaded through her damp hair.

A warning resounded in her mind, something about the cool water. Something she should remember…

But she didn't want to wake up from this dream. She

wanted to see where it would lead and what her lover would do to her.

His mouth closed over her breast, wet and demanding. She arched hard, the exquisite pleasure tormenting her. He explored her flesh as if he wanted to taste every inch of her.

And God help her, she wanted him to. It had been six years since her husband had visited her bed, but William's touches had been rough, never arousing like this. She kept her eyes closed, afraid this dream would vanish in the morning light, and all of it would end.

Juliana held his head to her breast as he suckled and teased, his other hand reaching over to caress her breast's twin. Between her thighs, she grew wet, and was startled that it had happened so easily. On the nights William had come to her bed, she'd lain naked beneath the coverlet, struggling to feel something.

She'd even touched herself a time or two before his visit, hoping to arouse herself. Anything that would make the lovemaking more comfortable and prevent her husband from criticizing her. But this dream was breaking past her meager knowledge of sex, leading her into so much more.

Again, a part of her grew fearful. As if she had to awaken, right now.

The fur beneath her had grown so hot, perspiration beaded upon her skin. She struggled to pull off the outer coverlet, and felt instead the length of a male body. Conjured from her imagination, this man was firm, with taut muscles. Juliana traced his chest, her hands exploring by touch. Her lover was powerful, with broad shoulders that tapered down to a lean waist.

My, but her imagination had selected an excellent specimen.

His hips were hardened muscles, and she marveled as she learned his body in the darkness, moving her hands over his heavy thighs. His erection rested against her stomach, thick and hard. Out of curiosity, she took it in her hand, and he let out a low growl as if he liked it.

The dream shifted, and his mouth lowered from her breasts, down to her ribs. He tilted her hips up, kissing a path down to her intimate flesh.

She started to protest, for this was something she'd never imagined. She wasn't at all sure he should—

Dear God above. His mouth feasted upon her, his tongue sliding within her moist entrance. Inside, her body shook with tremors, her breath seizing at the shocking sensations. She'd never imagined anything like this, and it took an effort to ignore the warnings in her mind.

She was shuddering, her fingers clenching at the fur while white-hot tendrils of desire drove her mad with need. He teased at the hooded flesh, provoking her toward the sensual pleasure she wanted so badly. And when she leaned into him, surrendering to her own needs, he suddenly pulled away.

Frustrated and upset, Juliana tried to bring him back, but instead, he replaced his mouth with the pressure of his fingers. The sensation was different, and when his mouth returned to her nipple, she felt the urgency roaring back.

Juliana leaned in, gripping his muscled shoulders as her body reveled in the glory of being touched this way. Instinctive tremors rocked her and she gripped his head as he forced her over the edge, a soaring heat of release pouring through her. Nothing in all the months of her marriage could have prepared her for the way her body craved his invasion.

Did Eyker touch you like this? he demanded.

Who was Eyker? Juliana struggled to open her eyes.

The dark warning inside her was gaining momentum, urging her to wake up. Something was wrong.

It would have been like this between us, if you had allowed it.

He moved against her throat, speaking words she didn't understand. Between her legs, she felt his blunt erection probing. Her body was wet, aching to be filled by this man. She wanted to forget everything, to lose herself in a dream of pleasure. Abruptly, she gasped as his slick heat filled her. This was what she'd wanted from William. This desperate need to be taken and to shatter the boundaries between them.

Though she couldn't understand how her mind had created this fantasy, she wasn't about to lie quietly and let the dream disappear. No, she gripped him hard, meeting his thrusts while she arched her hips to receive him. There was nothing polite or quiet about the lovemaking—it was carnal lust, almost savage in nature. She grew molten as he sheathed himself. A part of her half-expected this lover to be barbaric, to thrust in a rhythm that would hurt.

But instead, he seemed to know when to quicken the tempo and when to slow down. She was frantic for another climax, desperate to make this man shatter in the way she had. The boat was moving, and the rocking motion echoed the surges of his hips against hers.

Within her, she sensed him seeking his own release, and she wrapped her legs around his waist, holding fast as he rode her. A cry ripped from her mouth as he held her bottom and penetrated over and over. She was coming apart, her body shuddering against the rhythmic pleasure, until the release shot through her in mindless lust. When her nails scored the man's back, he let out his own groan, his hard body growing slack against hers.

Juliana kept her eyes closed, stunned that she'd

created such a vision in her mind. No doubt once she awakened, she would find herself back at home in her bed, with no man to share it.

It was a dream, and when dawn came, it would end.

Sparse rays of sunlight speared his eyes, and Arik blinked at the brightness. Although the morning air was cool against his bare skin, the woman in his arms was warm. His shaft hardened instantly, and he reached between her legs to prepare her, wanting the honeyed wetness against his fingertips. But when he rolled her over, his hands stilled upon her flesh. It wasn't Svala he'd taken last night. It was a woman he'd never seen before.

Uneasiness slid through him, and Arik wondered what was happening. Was she a slave girl, sent by Freya to tempt him? Was this a part of the afterlife? With his knuckles, he gently touched her skin. It prickled with gooseflesh, and she murmured something in her sleep. He didn't understand her words, and from the shape of her face, he guessed she was Anglo-Saxon. Yet the language was still foreign to his ears.

"Awaken," he commanded.

Her gray eyes flew open, and she let out a scream of terror. Gripping the furs to cover her nakedness, she looked horrified.

She started speaking words in a language he couldn't grasp, flustered words of panic and embarrassment. Her cheeks turned bright red, as if she'd suddenly remembered her actions from the night before. Arik folded his arms across his chest, waiting for her to speak words that made sense. When she gave none, he demanded, "Who are you?"

Her eyes narrowed, as if she'd suddenly understood his question. "You're...not English," she whispered. Her face furrowed as she spoke.

He didn't know what she was talking about, but he reached for his fallen clothing and covered himself. "I am called Arik Thorgrim, a *jarl* from the Ryger tribe."

"A what?"

"A *jarl*. I have lands in Rogaland, and my brother has settlements in East Anglia and Dubh Linn." He reached down and tossed her the discarded garment she'd worn the night before. It was a finely woven gown, one that spoke of her status. This woman was not a slave, but possibly a freewoman or a king's daughter. And yet, she wore no jewelry, save a small gold ring upon one hand. There were no jeweled torques nor bracelets to show her rank. He frowned, trying to determine more about her.

"What is your name? And what happened to your ship?" he demanded. If her family was searching for her, he would see to it that she was returned to them.

"I am Juliana Arthur, the Viscountess Hawthorne," she answered in his language, her eyes wide. "My father's ship broke free of its moorings, and the wind carried me out to sea. It was my own fault for climbing inside the boat."

"Then the gods did bring you to me." He studied her. "Clothe yourself and then we will talk further." Right now, he couldn't grasp what had happened. Though she wasn't Svala, her features were similar enough.

The sun had risen higher, casting light over the land nearby. It resembled the shores of East Anglia, but strange dwellings rested within the hills. He'd never seen anything like them, and more and more, he wondered if this was part of the afterlife.

There was no sign of Asgard, nor the Hall of Valhalla,

as he'd expected. Arik sat upon one of the benches, resting his hands upon the oars. Was this a test? Since he'd been murdered instead of dying in battle, did he have to earn his place among the warriors?

Perhaps he truly *had* heard the words *not yet.* He didn't understand any of it, and the gods weren't known to explain themselves to mortals.

"Take me home," Juliana pleaded. He turned and saw that her gray gown was still damp, the fabric outlining her slender body and rounded breasts. It reminded him of the night they'd spent together and the way she'd welcomed him into her arms.

She hadn't been afraid of him then. He'd touched her, believing she was Svala. And though he didn't know why this woman had allowed a stranger into her bed, nothing had been done against her will. He remembered the way she'd clenched his head, arching against him as he'd tasted her swollen flesh.

His body hardened at the memory, but he forced it back. Clearly, there were reasons why the woman had given herself but now held regrets.

She was shivering hard, the gown doing little to shield her from the wind. He returned to their sleeping place and brought out a heavy fur. When he advanced toward her, she took a step backward. He let her retreat, ignoring her fear as he wrapped the fur around her shoulders.

"You live there?" he questioned, pointing toward the land.

"Yes." She held on to the edges of the fur, still staring at him.

"Then I will guide the ship to the shore. You will grant me food and shelter in return."

Her gray eyes turned suspicious. "There's no place for

you at my house. I barely have a bed for my maid and my son."

A tension pulled at him when she mentioned a boy. "Where is your husband?"

She reddened. "I haven't seen him in six years. I think he's dead."

The traces of fear in her voice made him now understand her apprehension about the night they'd spent together. "And do you believe this?"

She lifted her shoulders in a shrug. "I don't know what to believe. But last night I was asleep... I never meant to—" Crestfallen, she stared at her feet, as if humiliated by what they'd done.

Arik took the fur covering with both hands, pulling her to stand closer to him. "I thought you were Svala, the woman who was promised as my bride."

Guilt stained her cheeks, but she raised her eyes to his. "What I did was wrong, and it won't happen again."

In her voice, he heard the firm resolution, and it irritated him that she'd dismissed him like a mistake to be swept aside. There was no doubt in his mind that he'd brought her pleasure last night, and by the gods, he wasn't without honor. He would never take a woman without her consent. But he wasn't at all averse to tempting her.

"It might." To remind her of it, he tilted her chin up and kissed her. It was a kiss of possession, to place a claim upon her. But when he tasted the softness of her lips, he gentled his mouth upon hers. Her hands dug into his shoulders, as if to protest. But he caught her against his chest, pulling her closer. And whether or not she wanted to kiss him, she yielded to him like a temptation she couldn't have.

If her husband were alive, Arik would have

understood her reluctance and honored it. But six years was too long to leave a woman like this behind. He had no doubt at all that her husband was dead.

Abruptly, she shoved him back, breaking the kiss. Her face flushed and she reminded him, "I have to go back to my son." She moved as far away from him as she could, and he saw the way her hands were shaking.

Arik moved to adjust the mainsail, then returned to the rudder, turning the vessel to make use of the wind. "Come here, Juliana of Arthur. Hold this steady."

She eyed him, but he stood firm on his order. He needed her help to steer the boat properly. After a moment, she climbed over the rows of benches until she reached the stern. Her face was pale, her lips swollen from his kiss. "You'll keep your word to bring me home to my son?"

"Yes." He stood and held out the rudder, guiding her hands. Juliana sat with her posture straight, not looking at him as she held the wood. She looked as lost as he felt. But he would bring her back to her home and learn whether or not she was telling the truth.

The path of his life had taken an unexpected turn. Never had he been given any reason to doubt his place in Valhalla. But…what if he wasn't truly dead? What if there was another purpose for him now?

He took his place on the bench, rowing toward the shore. Behind him, she remained silent. He glanced at the woman, and her expression held worry before she flushed at the memory of last night. Unlike Svala, she seemed embarrassed, as if she'd never expected to feel pleasure.

The memory of her passionate moans, the fervid touch of her hands, made him want to toss the oars aside and claim her body once again. But he understood her need to return to her son.

"Who are you really?" she interrupted, when he continued his rowing. "Did Marcus send you?"

"I know of no man named Marcus." He glanced back and saw the consternation lined upon her face.

"You're dressed like no one I've seen before, and you're speaking a language that I haven't heard since my maid, Grelod, taught it to me." Her fists curled at her hips. "What is it you want from me?"

He pulled the oars against the current, bringing them as close to the shore as he dared. "I might ask the same of you. You tempted me in your arms last night, trying to ensnare me before I could reach Valhalla in Asgard."

"I don't know what you're talking about. I nearly drowned last night."

"Or the gods brought you to me." He released the oars and stood before her. "Our fates are intertwined, so it seems."

"No, they aren't," she argued. "I've been through enough without needing another man to make me into a fool."

He sent her a dark look. "You should be grateful that I am willing to return you to your home instead of keeping you as my *thrall*."

She frowned. "I have no idea what you're talking about, but no man will keep me from my son." There was a cool tone to her voice that held a warning.

Arik moved to the bow of his ship and dropped the anchor near the dock. Juliana let go of the rudder and stood with her shoulders back, walking toward him as if he were her slave instead of the other way around. She reminded him of a Norsewoman, strong in her demeanor.

But she was sorely mistaken if she believed he was going to let her go. Somehow, she was tied to his fate. And he wouldn't rest, until he learned what his purpose was.

ChAPTER TWO

After the boat was secure upon its moorings, Juliana allowed Arik Thorgrim to lift her to the dock. His hands lingered upon her a moment too long, and his touch made her nervous.

"Thank you for your assistance, Mr. Thorgrim." She clasped her hands together, trying to distance herself from him, like a proper English widow. Not at all like a woman who had been intimate with a stranger.

The very thought set her cheeks on fire. She still couldn't believe that the dream had been real. She wasn't at all a woman of sensual desires. Hadn't William told her, time and again, what a disappointment she was? The day after their wedding, he'd told her that she needed to respond better to him, to grow aroused simply by looking at him.

But he'd had little effect on her—unlike this man, whose physical form reminded her of a Greek statue. He was tall, with broad shoulders, and she'd felt his ridged abdomen last night. His strong thighs had held not a trace of softness, like a warrior who had come off a battlefield.

His face seemed familiar somehow, and she tried to think of where she might have met this man. Long dark hair hung below his shoulders, and his brown eyes held interest, as if he remembered what they'd done last night. A stubble of beard lined his cheeks, and she thought of the way it had abraded her breasts as he'd licked and suckled her.

The thought sent a thrill through her body, making her respond against her will. No, she couldn't let herself be seduced again. The sooner she escaped his company, the better.

"Thank you for bringing me home. Now I'll bid you a good day." She nodded in dismissal and turned to leave.

"You will go nowhere without me, woman," came his reply.

Oh won't I? She stared at the man, disbelieving that he would have the gall to order her around. But he stepped out of the boat and tied it to the dock. It was a strange vessel, one that resembled a longboat from long ago. She hadn't seen anything like it. At the prow of the boat, there was a carved female face and a bronze weather vane.

Mr. Thorgrim strode across the dock until he reached her side. She suddenly realized how very large he was. Though she was taller than most women, the top of her head barely reached his mouth. Her eyes made direct contact with his muscled shoulders, forcing her to look up.

He wasn't dressed like anyone she'd ever seen. His woolen tunic was dun-colored, made in a primitive fashion. He wore darker trousers, a fur mantle across his shoulders, and leather braces upon his forearms. His dark eyes stared down at her with a hunger that made her shiver. He walked onto the shore with confidence, his leather boots striding through the sand. At his waist hung a long sword and a battle-ax. Arik Thorgrim almost reminded her of a…a Viking.

Strange to imagine it.

Her dog, Bartholomew, came dashing from the house, barking when he saw them. Behind him came Harry, but Grelod caught the boy in her arms before he could break free. The older woman's eyes widened as she spied the man at Juliana's side.

"Mama!" Harry shouted. "Where were you? And who is that?"

"Your mother went for a walk, as I told you," Grelod interrupted. "And found someone, I see." Strangely, the woman didn't seem at all worried or surprised that Juliana had been gone all night.

"It's a long story." She didn't know how to explain any of it, but it could wait until later. She opened her arms, and Harry came running into them. Relief flooded through her that she'd made it home safely to her son. She lifted him up, embracing him hard until he squirmed to get down. Mr. Thorgrim kept his distance, making it clear that he intended no harm to either of them. And though she ought to be relieved by that, his presence threatened her in a different way. He was so unlike any of the gentlemen she'd ever met—so bold and domineering. It had been all too easy to succumb to the reckless desire he'd kindled, surrendering herself to needs she hadn't known were there.

"Who is that?" Harry demanded, staring at the man. "He looks like a beggar."

"Hush, now." Juliana touched her son's mouth. "That isn't a polite thing to say." While Mr. Thorgrim did indeed resemble a beggar, her son needed to mind his manners.

Harry tilted his head back to stare at the stranger. Thorgrim crossed his arms over his chest as if inspecting her son, in turn. While the man's expression was unyielding, his demeanor softened in front of the boy. Almost as if he'd remembered a child's curiosity.

Bartholomew was jumping up, still barking, and the man knelt, resting his palm upon the dog's head. Immediately, the animal quieted.

"Are you magic?" Harry breathed. He seemed enchanted at the prospect.

"His name is Mr. Thorgrim," Juliana said. "And he does not speak English." She touched Harry's hair and murmured, "Go on now, back into the house." But her son didn't move, for he was fascinated by the stranger.

Already she could see that Thorgrim was studying her house as if he believed he ought to stay here with her. She had to dissuade him of that notion as soon as possible. But before she could speak, he reached out to his belt and withdrew a knife. Now what was he doing with that? The iron blade gleamed in the morning sun, and it looked sharp enough to slice through paper. He eyed Harry and then offered him the knife, hilt first.

"What are you doing?" Juliana demanded in his language.

"It is a gift, in thanks for your hospitality. Your son does not have a blade of his own, so I will give him mine."

"He's five years old!' Juliana protested. "He doesn't need a knife."

"Then how will he learn to defend himself? Or hunt?" Thorgrim nodded permission, and Harry reached out toward the hilt.

"You will not touch that knife," Juliana said, pushing it away. The longer she spent time in this man's company, the more she realized how uncivilized he was. What sort of person would give a five-year-old boy a deadly blade? She knew almost nothing about him, except that he behaved like a barbarian and…and he'd driven her mad with his touch. Almost as if he'd bewitched her into becoming a different woman.

She had to make him leave as soon as possible.

After guiding Harry behind her, ordering him back to the house, Juliana squared her shoulders and faced down Mr. Thorgrim. "I am grateful to you for bringing me home. And I hope you will have a safe journey back to…wherever you came from."

Her words did not have the impact she anticipated. His face grew shielded, his mouth frowning. "Is there no man to protect your household?"

She stiffened. "I do not need a man to keep my son safe."

Thorgrim took a step closer. "If you have no man, then I will stay with you this night." He eyed her damp gown. "For you are not safe without someone to stand guard."

"You will not." The words escaped her with more force than she'd intended. "I mean, there is no need. You—"

But he was already striding toward the door, with Harry standing at the entrance. Juliana clenched her arms around her chest, watching over her son. He appeared to be talking to Thorgrim, while the man stood in the doorway, observing the interior of the small house.

She was about to follow, but Grelod stepped in her path. The older woman stared at Juliana and demanded, "Where did *he* come from?"

"He saved my life last night when I was pulled out to sea." She started to go after the pair of them, but Grelod held her back. A strange expression came over the woman's face.

"Then he is the answer you've been seeking," the old

woman warned. "I can sense the spirits surrounding him. You must keep him."

Keep him? It wasn't as if the man were a stray dog. And what did she mean, *the answer you've been seeking*? The only answer Juliana needed was a way out of this poverty. And judging from this man's demeanor and appearance, he was *not* a duke in disguise. More like a beggar who had washed up on shore.

A very handsome, tantalizing beggar, who had known exactly how to touch her last night.

Juliana's face flushed scarlet when she remembered what she'd allowed this man to do to her while she was dreaming. More and more, she felt as if she'd fallen beneath a spell. Caught up in her dreams, she'd surrendered to his seduction. It bothered her that a stranger would affect her so violently, giving her the greatest sexual pleasure she'd ever experienced. It was the *only* desire she'd ever known, if the truth be told.

No, he didn't belong here. And the sooner she bid him farewell, the better.

She closed her eyes, shaking off the wayward thoughts. "I have no intention of 'keeping him,' as you say." Juliana stepped past her, toward the door. "I'll speak with him, and then hopefully, he'll sail off to wherever he came from."

As she passed her maid, the matron began muttering under her breath in Norwegian. It sounded as if she was casting a magic spell, for Juliana caught words about a summoning, and something about the moon and the goddess. A chill prickled over her spine, for she *had* sensed an otherworldly moment, a few hours ago.

Juliana opened the door to her house and saw her son standing, pointing to one object after another. "Chair," he said, pointing to the wooden seat.

"Chair," Arik repeated. He was listening intently to her son, repeating back every word Harry spoke.

"You said he can't speak English, Mama," Harry reminded her. "But I'm teaching him to talk."

Juliana ignored her son's declaration and demanded in Norwegian, "What are you doing, Thorgrim?"

"As your son said. Learning your language." He pointed to several objects around the room and named each one in English. When his hand touched the chair, he moved his fingers over the curved wood. "Did your husband make this?"

She shook her head. "My father did." A wave of sadness came over her, for his death had come so swiftly. He might have been a humble fisherman, but a wiser man she'd never met. She missed him dearly.

Thorgrim seemed to sense her sadness and offered, "He was skilled." Glancing around the house, he studied the interior intently, before his gaze fixed upon her son. In his eyes, she saw a storm of emotions. Then, abruptly, he left the house, returning outside.

Instinct warned her to stay in one place, but she had no idea what the man might do next. "Stay here, Harry," she told him. "Open your primer, and read aloud to Grelod. I'll be back in a few moments." She set down the fur covering she'd wrapped around her shoulders and replaced it with a spare woolen cloak, since her other cloak was now at the bottom of the sea.

Outside, she closed the door behind her and hurried to follow Thorgrim. His pace was swift as he climbed the hillside behind the house, his movement fluid and strong. It was a struggle to catch up to him on the narrow path, but she hastened forward.

When they stood at the top of the hill, he shielded his eyes against the sun and stared out at the sea. Trouble and fury brewed within him, and she wondered if it had been a mistake to follow him.

He made no acknowledgement of her presence but sat down upon a large granite boulder. For a long time, his gaze remained upon the sea and on his ship anchored in the harbor. "This is not Asgard," he said at last. "I am caught between worlds."

She kept a safe distance away, not understanding. "What do you mean?" The look in his eyes was of a man lost. Beneath his fierce demeanor, she saw a glimmer of uncertainty.

"I do not know why I was summoned here," he answered. "Or why you were sent to me."

"I—I wasn't sent to you," she protested. "I told you, the wind carried my ship out to sea."

"So you say." He stood up and drew nearer. "I was killed in battle, a day ago. Why am I not dead?"

The intensity in his voice frightened her. His words were of a madman, incomprehensible. She took another step backward, a harsh chill rising over her skin. He believed this, didn't he? And that made him dangerous.

Before she could flee, he pulled her back from the edge of the path, his hands closing around her waist. "Are you an evil spirit, sent by Freya to tempt me from the afterworld? Is that why you gave yourself to me?" He gripped her closer, until her body merged against his.

Fear seized her mind, but her body was well aware of the hard lines of this man. He was ruthless and without mercy.

And yet, she sensed that he was also afraid.

"I am not a spirit," she said calmly. "You seduced me while I was unconscious. I didn't know what was happening."

"You were willing. And eager."

She shook her head, her heartbeat stumbling within her chest. It had been a dream, one that had pulled her from the harsh reality of life and had given her a moment of forbidden pleasure.

His hands moved down to her hips, drawing her nearer. "Are you a witch?"

"No." The whisper was barely audible, and he bent his face to hers. His heated breath warmed her cheek, and he brought his hands to cradle her face.

"Admit that you are a test from the gods." His mouth nipped at hers, as if to coax the truth from her lips. Though his kiss was only meant to provoke her, she felt the pull of temptation. And she could not dare tread upon that path toward sin.

"I am nothing more than a woman trying to protect her son. I don't know who you are or what any of this means." Emotion tightened inside her, and she wished he would simply leave.

Her words hung between them, and he drew back to regard her. "I saw things in your home. Things that are not of this world. A likeness of a woman that could be drawn by no human hands."

He was speaking of the oil portrait of her mother, she realized. But how could he think it was not of this world?

He gripped her shoulders in an unmistakable warning. "Tell me what place this is, woman. When I sailed away from land, a storm took my ship and brought me here."

"This is…England," she whispered. "I don't know what you—"

"When?" he demanded. "The seasons are different. It was summer when I left."

"It's February," she whispered. "February of 1811."

His face was harsh, like a stone battered by the sea.

"You lie to me, woman." His hands tightened over her shoulders. "Do not believe I am a fool."

A liar, was she? This had gone too far.

Juliana shoved him back with all of her strength. "Why would I lie to you? I hardly know you at all. You saved my life, and I have offered my gratitude for that. But since then, you've done nothing but order me around." Her own anger surged, for she didn't deserve his fury. "You can believe whatever you wish, but I've spoken the truth."

She turned her back on him and began walking home. The man was impossible, clearly angry and half-potted. But a moment later, she heard his footsteps behind her.

"Wait."

She didn't know what it was that made her stop, but she heard the note of fear in his voice. "What is it?" Still, she remained with her back to him.

"You said...it is the year 1811?"

"Yes."

"You are certain of this?"

She did turn around then. "My son was born in September of 1805. Of course I am certain."

Thorgrim's face whitened, but he held his ground. "Then I am cursed, it seems. For I was supposed to die a thousand years ago."

"There's no such thing as a curse." Although his clothing did resemble a Viking's, she refused to believe that a man could cross through time. Such a thing was impossible.

Just as it was impossible for a boat to pull her out to sea without anyone commanding it. Or to drift miles from shore within a matter of minutes.

A chill settled inside her veins, for she could see that he believed it.

"But there is a curse, Juliana of Arthur. And now, I must learn how to break it."

The young woman standing before him had doubt in her eyes. She didn't at all believe that a thousand years had passed. But Arik knew. Somehow, he'd known, from the first moment sunlight had illuminated her clothing, that she was not of his world—or of his time. Juliana was unlike the other women he'd met. Perhaps she was a blooded descendant of Svala, meant to haunt him in death. Or perhaps the mischievous god Loki had rewoven time, bringing them together.

He let her walk away while he sat back upon the stone to think. Somehow, he believed that Juliana was the key to unlocking his journey to immortality. His death had not brought him to Valhalla; instead, it had brought him to her.

He couldn't understand what he was meant to do. Her home was fine enough, though it needed repairs. It would be easy to provide her with food and protection. But any man could give her the same. As beautiful as she was, it would not be difficult for her to find a guardian. He remembered her soft body and the way it had curved into him, welcoming him with warmth and passion. Beneath her cool dignity lay a woman of intensity who had given him a night he'd not soon forget.

Arik stood up and continued down the path, intending to bring home fish to feed them. It did not appear that Juliana had stored enough to survive the rest of the winter. He walked down the narrow pathway toward the sea and saw her standing upon the sand, staring out at the gray water. Unhappiness cloaked her demeanor, the lines of worry creasing her face. She watched her son emerge from the house, and he laughed as he ran along the shore. Harry was chased by the older woman, who began scolding him. Juliana watched the pair, and the worry in her eyes was evident. She did love the boy. There was a gentleness there, her eyes softening while she watched him.

He continued walking until he reached her side. "If you have nets, I will go and bring back fish for your family this night."

She nodded. "My father has some nets." She told him where to find them, but then added, "But it isn't necessary. I have bread and some vegetables. We'll be fine."

He saw that she was still looking at her son. "Something troubles you about your boy. Is there a threat I should know of? Has an enemy attacked?"

A rueful smile lifted her mouth. "In a way. But it's not an enemy either of us can fight. My husband's brother claims that my son is a bastard and has taken the lands that were entailed to Harry."

"Would you like me to kill him for you?"

She laughed, though he'd been serious in the offer. "You can't go and kill a man just because he stole an inheritance. I've been seeking help from solicitors, and—"

"If he is dead, the land is yours for the taking." Arik began to glimpse the possibilities. If he had to prove his bravery in battle, this might be the means. Once he had slain her enemy, the gods might grant him the right to spend eternity with the other warriors. His gaze settled upon the young boy. For a child, he had shown no fear. Harry was inquisitive and it was likely that the boy could be taught to be a strong fighter. Arik could understand Juliana's need to guard him.

"You will show me the lands your son has lost," he demanded. "We will hire warriors to help us, and I will see that he is restored to what is rightfully his."

Juliana shook her head. "If you try to take Hawthorne House by force, you'll end up in prison or hanged for it. I do appreciate your offer, however." Her hands moved around her waist as if she could press the fear back inside her. "Still, this is my battle to face."

"By hiding in your father's house?"

"I'm not hiding. It's just that…finding the evidence takes time. Once I've proven that my marriage was legal, I can be the viscountess once more."

From her tone, it sounded like she was trying to avoid her enemy. Arik preferred a more direct approach, but he didn't doubt that he could achieve the same results. He would learn more about her enemy and later decide how to help her.

"I will go fishing and take the boy with me," he offered. "He's old enough to learn."

As he'd predicted, Juliana was already shaking her head with refusal. "No. He can't swim and he might fall overboard."

"I would never let him drown. My own father took me on his boat as soon as I could walk." A sudden ache caught him at the memory, knowing that he would never see Valdr again. They had fought bitterly when Arik had left, and he wished he could go back and change what he'd said. He had thoughtlessly told his father that he never wanted to see him again—and now he never would. Regret curled within him at the thought.

"You cannot take Harry with you," Juliana insisted. "You're a stranger to me, and I'm not about to let my son go off with a man who claims he is over a thousand years old."

His temper flared up, that she would treat him like one whose mind had wandered away. Words of denial rose to his lips, but instead of voicing them, he offered, "Then come with us to guard him as you will. What harm is there?"

"Last night, I nearly drowned. There's a great deal of harm."

"And I saved you," he pointed out. His tone deepened as he thought of her bare skin against his. "I warmed you with my own flesh."

She paled at the memory, and her voice came out in a whisper. "What happened between us was a mistake."

"Was it?" He took her hand in his and drew it to his chest. "Or was it our fate?" Her palm was delicate beneath his, her gray eyes filled with doubt.

Before she could protest again, he added, "We shall make a wager on it. You and the boy will go out on the boat with me, and we will see who brings in the most fish. If you win the wager, I am yours to command. If I win—" He let his voice drift away, letting her imagination conjure the rest.

"I will not be yours to command," she said emphatically.

"Not yet, Juliana. But there will come a time when you will want what I have to offer."

Her cheeks flushed, though he'd been speaking of his protection. Though he did not know why the gods had summoned him into her world, he believed that helping her was necessary to winning his immortality. This woman was alone with no one to guard her, and her lands had been taken. If he conquered her enemies, surely that would be enough to lift whatever curse had brought him here. He could prove that he was a warrior of strength and bravery, one who deserved to be with the gods.

"I want you to leave," she said. "There is no need for a wager."

He made her nervous—he could see it in her eyes. But the wager was merely an excuse to remain at her side. "I cannot leave until I learn why I was brought to you. My afterlife depends on it."

He was convinced that he was trapped between worlds, between the immortality he wanted and the mortal world of a thousand years later. Somehow he had been found unworthy to enter Asgard to celebrate with the gods in Valhalla. And whether it was Odin watching over him or whether this was a trick of Loki, he was certain that he was meant to aid this woman.

Disbelief clouded her eyes. Before she could voice another protest, he added, "You cannot force me to leave. But I am willing to put my trust in the gods. If you win the wager, then I will leave and not trouble you again. If the gods grant me the victory, then you will allow me to fight on your behalf."

Juliana didn't look pleased about the wager, but she seemed to consider it. "If I win, do you promise to go?"

"I will." He had no qualms about the vow, for he had no doubt he would win. "But after I win, I will stay with you through the phases of this moon," he said. "And I will get back the land that was stolen from you and your son. Be assured of it."

She shook her head. "You cannot kill Marcus."

He made no reply to that. "Tell your son of the wager, and I will prepare the boat."

The sea was calm, and Mr. Thorgrim helped Harry and her to climb aboard his ship. Her son chattered without ceasing, as he peppered the man with questions about sailing and fishing. Juliana did her best to translate, and was glad to see that not once did Thorgrim seem impatient about answering the child.

As they traveled farther out to sea, she helped him adjust the sails, until the ship picked up speed. The look of excitement on Harry's face made her wish she'd taken him out sooner. The wind whipped at his dark hair, and his eyes drank in the sight of the land skimming past.

When at last Thorgrim gathered up the nets, he showed Harry how to cast them out. He guided the boy's hands, and at the sight of them together, a sense of regret pulled at her heart. Harry had never known a father. He'd never had a man to show him anything at all, and even his grandfather had died before he was old enough to know him. But Arik Thorgrim had slid into the role seamlessly.

For a man who believed he was over a thousand years old, he didn't behave like a madman. And when he pulled in his net, filled with fish, the challenging look on his face dared her to beat him.

She couldn't believe her own net was empty while his was full. They were on opposite sides of the same boat. It wasn't as if she'd never cast nets out before—her father had taught her to fish, when she was a young girl. She *knew* how to do this.

It was almost as if the ocean were conspiring against her. She tried. Oh, how she tried, racking her brain for every ounce of knowledge her father had imparted. But even the one fish she pulled in from her net was hardly large enough to keep. The smirk on Mr. Thorgrim's face made her all the more determined to catch more, but every time she cast it out, there was nothing.

"It's not over yet," she warned.

"I've caught thirty-two fish." He set the net down at

his feet and rested his hands on his knees. "Do you want me to continue, so that you will have more to store for the rest of the winter?"

The thought of cleaning all the fish made her wince. She didn't want to admit defeat, but there seemed to be no other choice. Then, too, she feared living under the same roof as this man, for he tempted her in ways William never had.

Raising her eyes to his, she lifted her hands in surrender. "Stop. We'll never be able to eat all of these. We should release them."

"You will need most of them until spring," he corrected, "but we may release some of them."

He placed a wriggling fish into Harry's hands, and the boy beamed with delight. One by one, they tossed the smaller fish back into the sea, keeping half of the catch for their own. The sun had already drifted downward into late afternoon, and when they sailed back, Harry curled up to sleep on a fur resting upon the bottom of the ship.

"He had a long day," she murmured. "But it meant a great deal to him."

Thorgrim tied back the sail and came to sit beside her. "You should be proud of the boy. Even if you did indulge him and treat him like a girl all these years."

"I never treated him like a girl." Why would he think that? She'd taught him his lessons each day, and Harry was wearing clothes befitting a five-year-old boy. He was well-mannered, though a trifle too enthusiastic at times.

"He doesn't know how to hunt, use a knife, or defend himself." Thorgrim nodded toward the sleeping boy. "You might as well put a gown on him."

Oh, for goodness' sake. She supposed this man would already be teaching Harry how to engage in fisticuffs.

"He doesn't need to know how to use a knife. I am raising him to be kind, intelligent, and polite."

"Like a girl."

She was about to make another retort, when she saw the teasing look in his eyes. "If you had your way, you'd be teaching him how to stab things."

"It is a useful skill." He shifted his weight, sitting closer to her. "I might also teach him how to treat women."

"You had better not!" she said, thinking of the night he'd seduced her. "He's only five."

"Women should be protected," he said quietly. "Do you disagree?"

Slowly, she shook her head. In his demeanor, she saw a man who believed in what he said. She didn't doubt that if any enemy attacked his woman, he would fight to the death for her. No one would threaten her with this man at her side, and the thought was strangely comforting. Still, she told him, "You don't have to fight my battles for me, Mr. Thorgrim."

"Arik," he corrected. "And you are wrong." He took her hand in his, bringing it to his face. Against her fingertips, she felt the rough texture of his beard, and she had to press back the flare of interest.

"I know not what brought me here, Juliana of Arthur," he said, kissing her fingertips. "But this world of yours is not so different from my own. There are enemies to fight, and children to guard." He leaned in, his hands sliding around her waist. "Women to touch."

She had to remind herself that he wasn't speaking the truth. He might believe he was from another era, but only a madman would speak as he did. And yet, there could be no doubt that he wanted to help her.

When she stared into his eyes, she saw a man who

would never stand down for a cause he believed in. No one had offered to help her before. But this stranger had promised to defend her and get back the lands she had lost.

A blush spread over her cheeks. "Why would you want to help me?"

"Because I believe, even if you do not, that I was brought here for a reason. If I give you the help you need, I may meet the fate I deserve in Valhalla. I will destroy any man who dares to take what belongs to you."

There was no doubt that he meant it. But she couldn't have this man attempting to kill Marcus, even if William's brother *had* taken Harry's inheritance.

"It's impossible," she argued. "If you stay with me, people will talk. They will accuse me of letting you into my bed."

"Your husband has abandoned you," he pointed out. "It is your right to take another protector."

She didn't believe that. William might have been gone for many years, but she could not set aside her marriage so easily. Especially after Marcus had claimed she was nothing more than William's mistress. She wasn't. She had spoken her vows before a clergyman and signed the register.

Her husband had not yet been declared legally dead, and she could not risk bringing another man into her life—even if he was trying to help her.

"I thought you were a woman who kept her word," he said. "But I can see upon your face that you do not intend to keep the wager."

She said nothing, though the guilt began to take root. *You cannot let him stay,* her conscience chided. It was madness to consider letting him interfere with her troubles. This was her mistake, and *she* should be the one

42

to find the answers. Not a man who claimed he was a thousand-year-old Viking. Any woman would be wary of accepting help from a stranger.

But then, he had taken them sailing today and had shown her son nothing but kindness. Despite his overbearing nature, she sensed that there was honor in him. And the truth was, as a woman, her rights were limited, and she could only do so much.

"I will keep my word to give you shelter for the night," she said slowly. "But you cannot take William's place."

"I already have." He adjusted the sail and moved to sit beside her. "I am your protector now. In all ways." The deep timbre of his voice reminded her of exactly how he had taken care of her...and the sensual way he'd touched her.

Juliana couldn't deny that she had enjoyed the night they'd spent together, though it had been sinful. "Being with you last night was a mistake," she whispered. "It won't happen again." If she behaved immorally, it would only add weight to Marcus's lies.

"It might," he answered. She was conscious of how close his body was pressed to hers, and she knew, too well, what it felt like to lie beneath him.

"We were brought together by the gods," he continued. "It is my fate to defend your son's inheritance. And once I have slain your enemies, I will have my reward."

Her eyes widened at the horrifying image of him wielding a battle-ax against her brother-in-law. "Truly, you don't need to slay anyone."

He ignored her words and reached out to one of the ropes, adjusting the sail. "Hold this with both hands."

She obeyed, the wind filling up the sail. Only then did

she realize that he'd trapped her, making it impossible for her to release the ropes. His arm closed around her shoulders. "I will do whatever I must to win this battle, Juliana."

She grew still, wondering if he intended to claim her as his conquest. Already she knew the wildness of being in his arms and succumbing to his touch. Somehow she had to stay away from this man.

As his mouth closed over hers, capturing her lips in another kiss, she realized just how difficult that would be.

CHAPTER THREE

He sensed her reticence as he tasted her lips again. They were as soft as cream, and he'd made no effort to resist the urge. Juliana was a beautiful woman, but she confused him. In his homeland, the women were forthright and honest. If they wanted a man, they told him so.

But although Juliana claimed she did not want him, she released the ropes and rested her hands upon his chest. She appeared torn between resisting him and allowing herself the desires she craved.

"I can't," she whispered. "Please don't ask this of me."

He ignored her plea. "Do not protect you? Then who will, Juliana of Arthur?"

Her hands were poised upon his heart as she stared beyond him at the sea. "I may have been seduced once. But that isn't the sort of woman I am." Closing her eyes, she admitted, "I'm ashamed of what I did. If anyone learns of it, it only makes their case against me stronger. Harry will suffer for it."

Her gaze centered upon her son, her face filled with worry. In her life, the boy's needs came first, while she sacrificed all else for him.

As his own mother might have done. Arik studied her with new eyes, wondering who this woman truly was and why he had been called to guard her. He released her, but her hands rested upon him a moment longer.

Her face held regret as she spoke. "I apologize if I led you to believe differently."

She had, but he said nothing of it. "When we return to shore, your slave should clean a few fish for our dinner and preserve the rest for your winter." At least he could ensure that they wouldn't starve. Though Juliana might be capable of catching more fish, her earlier efforts had borne little fruit.

"Grelod is not a slave. She helps me with Harry," Juliana explained. "And she has been my companion for many years."

Arik continued guiding the boat back to shore, and Harry woke up just as they arrived. He chattered happily, and though he tried to understand the boy's dialect, it was beyond him to make sense of it. Even so, just being around the child brought a warmth to his heart. He'd always wanted a son of his own.

He gave the boy a smaller basket of fish to carry, and Harry proudly marched beside him. Arik hefted the remainder, holding his own basket on one shoulder. When they reached the dwelling, he took a closer look at the structure. The wood had aged, and no one had bothered to repair the holes. No doubt it was freezing at night with most of the heat escaping.

"If you prepare our meal, I will seal up the cracks in your house."

Juliana looked startled at the offer. "You needn't, really. We'll manage."

Did she think him incapable of it? He eyed her with a hard stare. "No woman or child should live in a house this ill-protected from the wind. I intend to change that."

Without waiting for her answer, he set down the basket in front of the door and left.

Arik mixed thick mud and clay that he'd brought back from a source farther inland. It had been difficult to dig it up, for the ground was cold and partially frozen. With the help of water, he managed to create a blend that would seal off the crevices. The young boy had followed, and he'd given Harry two empty buckets to carry. After they filled the containers with the clay and mud, Arik had carried the buckets back, since they were too heavy for the child to lift.

The child continued to speak words he didn't recognize, but from his tone, Arik recognized the boy's words as questions. It struck him as unusual that the boy would not have learned the Norse language, since both his mother and her handmaiden spoke it. In the end, he decided that speaking was unnecessary. It was easier to demonstrate to Harry how to repair the cracks in the walls.

When he reached the far side of the house, he lifted a handful of mud and smoothed it into one of the open crevices in the wall. The boy came closer and pointed to the earthen mixture. "Mud?" he asked.

Arik nodded and placed a handful in the boy's palm. He guided Harry to fill in the cracks, and as his larger hands covered the boy's smaller ones, regret spilled over him. Had he lived, he might have sired a son such as this. He could have trained him in the ways his father had taught him, showing him how to sail and hunt.

But he would never have a son if he was truly dead.

A pang of loss filled him at the realization that he had no future remaining. Only the gods knew why he had been sent here. Perhaps it was not for Juliana but for the boy.

Why had she remained here alone without her family? As far as he could tell, there were only the two women and Harry. His gaze shifted to the sea. Although they likely believed they were safe enough, he intended to move them from here as soon as possible. It was too easy for an invading fleet to sail upon these shores at dawn, attacking at first light. Juliana would become a prize of war, raped or enslaved, if she had no one to guard her. He could not let that happen.

Though he could repair the house to last them for a few months, he intended to bring them to a safer dwelling and help to conquer the lands that had been stolen.

The wind shifted, curling a chill over his spine as the sun grew lower in the sky. He was caught in a half life, a world between worlds. He didn't doubt that there was magic at play here, a test he had to face. It was like a dream, one from which he longed to awaken.

As he continued to spread the mud, a daydream caught him unawares. In the vision, he saw a man who resembled his father...and yet the man wore clothing that was different. He heard himself speaking a strange language he'd never encountered before, and while Arik daydreamed, he could almost imagine that he understood Harry's words.

"Will you be my new papa?" the child was asking.

He broke free of his dream, startled. Words came to his lips, but he knew not what they meant. He should not have understood the boy just now. The language Harry spoke was foreign, a tongue of the Anglo-Saxons.

And yet, for the slightest moment, he'd understood the boy's words. Unease filled him, for surely it was Loki's mischief at play.

The boy spoke again, and once more, his words became senseless chatter. Arik forced himself to pay closer heed to the task at hand, but the truth remained— there were visions in his mind that did not belong to him. He had seen this world through another man's eyes, heard a language through another man's ears.

It was a strange magic, one that made the hair stand up on the back of his arms.

When Juliana opened the door and saw them repairing her home, her face softened. "I told you, you didn't need to do that."

"It is cold at night, is it not?" He continued smoothing more mud into the cracks, trying to push away the uneasiness of the vision.

"Yes, but we'll find somewhere else to go, Mr. Thorgrim. I won't be keeping Harry here much longer. Once I've found the proof of my marriage, I'll return to my true home."

"With my help."

Her expression turned wary, as if she didn't trust him to succeed in this task. But he had gone a-viking many times in the past, and rarely had he failed. Nor would he fail in this.

He guided her son to fill another crevice, watching as the boy took pride in his work. Juliana winced at the mud on his hands, and Arik said, "I will help him wash after we have finished here."

The boy beamed at his mother and uttered words in their language, his tone filled with excitement.

"Both of you are covered in mud," she said. "I'll have Grelod heat water so you can bathe." She spoke to the boy in her own language, and the child grimaced as if he didn't want to wash.

Arik took a step nearer, watching the play of nervousness upon her face. The wind blew against her hair, tearing a few honeyed strands free of the knot she'd pinned up. He remembered the tangle of her wet hair against her shoulders while she'd embraced him against her bare skin.

"You could wash me as well," he said softly, "when all of them are asleep."

Juliana colored and took a step back. "No. Y-you'll be spending the night with the horses." She rubbed her shoulders, glancing down at the ground. "It might be a little cold in there, but it's all I have."

It was a lie. She could have invited him inside her own home, but it was clear that he intimidated her. Her gray eyes held wariness. "Or you could still leave."

He let the last of the mud fall from his fingertips. "Are you afraid of me, Juliana?"

She bit her lip and gave a single nod. "It isn't proper for you to be alone with us." She took Harry's hand in hers, but Arik took the boy's muddy palm before she could leave with him. He pointed toward the sea water, and with reluctance, Juliana allowed him to lead the boy there.

"In the morning, we will travel to your husband's home," he continued. "And we will take it back from your enemies."

In her eyes, he could see the shocked protests forming. "What do you mean—take it back? Hawthorne House isn't a fortress you can invade and simply conquer."

"But it is." He continued leading the boy down to the edge of the shore, and she followed, hurrying to keep up.

"You're just one man. There's nothing you can do," she pointed out.

Arik ignored her protests. She might doubt him, but there were mercenaries who would follow his bidding, no matter what sort of world this was.

He let go of the boy's hand and bent down to the salt water. It was freezing, numbing his skin as he washed. Arik showed the child how to wash the mud from his hands and forearms, but Harry didn't at all look eager to get clean.

"At dawn, we will ride out. The boy should stay here with the old woman, and you will show me the place that rightfully belongs to you," he told her.

Already she was shaking her head. "Mr. Thorgrim, no."

He didn't understand the title *Mister* that she kept calling him. "My name is Arik. And believe that I will not fail you in this."

She stared at him in disbelief, and he countered it by pressing her weakness. "Do you want your son to spend the remainder of the winter in a place like this?" He rested his hands upon the boy's shoulders. "Or would you rather see him warm and dry with enough food to eat?"

"It's not a good idea. Marcus could—"

"Does he live there, at Hawthorne House?"

"No, but he's taken possession of the property. The servants won't allow me anywhere near the grounds."

"We'll ride out in the morning and make our plans."

Juliana grew silent at that, looking doubtful. Arik knelt beside the boy and took Harry's hands in his. The boy yelped when he helped him dip his hands into the water, washing them.

"Yes, it is cold," he agreed, rinsing his own arms again from elbow to wrist. The boy put on a brave face and washed his hands a second time, shivering hard. Arik reached out to take Harry's hand but was startled when the boy hugged him. The impulsive gesture was unexpected, and it bothered him that this child had never known a father. He wasn't at all a person the boy should grow attached to. He was as good as dead, his spirit transported across time.

When this task was done, Arik didn't want the boy to feel abandoned. Better that he should keep his distance. Though it bothered him, he extricated the boy from his embrace and kept a stoic face as they returned to the house.

Juliana was beginning to understand exactly how Eve had felt when the serpent tempted her with the apple.

Arik stood near the fire with his back to the room. She'd given him a basin of warmed water and a towel to dry himself. He'd soaked the cloth in the water, and though she was helping Grelod bathe Harry, she couldn't stop herself from stealing glances at him. Stripped of his tunic, the broad-shouldered man had the most muscular form she'd ever seen.

Water rolled in heavy droplets down his bare skin, and as he reached back to wash, her mind drifted to the night they'd spent together. It was no wonder she'd believed he was a dream, for she'd never imagined any man could look like this. His face wasn't at all like the other men she'd known—charming and handsome. No, his held the scars of battle, his dark hair rough and wild. He seemed to sense that she was staring, and he turned toward her. His dark brown eyes held wickedness, and he let her look her fill.

Goodness, he really *did* seem like a Viking, foolish thought that it was.

The ridged muscles across his chest held a dusting of hair, while his abdomen was lean and firm. Her skin tightened against her gown, and Juliana hardly heard a word her maid was saying.

"Mama," Harry interrupted. "Isn't the house warmer? Did I do well, helping Mr. Thorgrim fix the cracks?"

"You did, son." She forced her attention back to the boy, who was shivering while Grelod dressed him in his nightclothes.

"Come and eat, both of you," Grelod urged, guiding them to the table. To Mr. Thorgrim, she said in Norwegian, "I want to speak with you alone. Out near the horses, where you'll be sleeping."

He eyed her maid with a discerning look and gave a shrug.

"Wait," Juliana said, before he could follow the older woman outside. His tunic was still wet from the sea water, and he needed something else to wear.

She rummaged through a trunk containing her father's clothes and brought over one of his shirts, as well as a coat. "These won't fit you well, but at least it will keep you warm." Holding it out to him, she saw the slight flare in his eyes, before he nodded his thanks. The sleeves were several inches above his wrists, but the garments were better than nothing.

After he left with Grelod, curiosity urged her to stand near the door, where she could eavesdrop on their conversation. "Hush, Harry," she told her boy, leaning against the wood. She overheard her maid speaking in Norwegian to the man, but the woman's words made little sense.

"The moon will complete its phases in a month," Grelod was saying. "Your time grows short."

"And how would you know this?"

"I know what you are. And I know from whence you came, Viking. I prayed to Freya on my lady's behalf, and the goddess summoned you here for her."

Summoned? Juliana frowned, not understanding what her maid meant by that.

"Was it you who kept me from my afterlife?" he demanded, his voice filled with fury.

"You did not wish to die, did you?" When Arik gave no answer, Grelod continued. "Juliana needs your help, and you were chosen by the gods for it. But such magic cannot last beyond the moon. I have foreseen it. Death will come, and a great reward awaits the one who makes the necessary sacrifice."

A silence descended between them, and a sudden chill came over her. Although Grelod had always believed in magic and foretelling the future, Juliana thought it was all nonsense. She only trusted what she could see or touch.

And yet, last night, there had been too many unexplained events. Hadn't her boat been swept out to sea, leaving her in danger of drowning? Every part of that night defied logic. Her father's boat was still missing, and a longboat was here in its place. The man who had come to her was primitive and domineering.

She could almost believe that he was conjured, not real. Like one of the Greek gods, brought down to earth to seduce a human woman. But could he be a Viking?

No. He reminded her of someone she had met, though she couldn't remember who. He was only a man—and a familiar one—not some lost soul summoned from another time.

And yet, her body had reveled in Arik's touch. She

could not forget his hands upon her skin, the aching sensuality of his body moving inside hers. The memory was raw enough to arouse her once again.

Stop this. She wouldn't allow herself to fall beneath that spell. Her mind shielded itself from thoughts of the impossible, as she turned back to her son. She distracted herself by serving Harry the fish Grelod had cooked, eating her own small portion.

When Thorgrim and her maid returned, she tried to behave as if she'd overheard nothing at all. But as she ate, she could feel his eyes upon her, watching. Juliana stole a few glances at him, noticing how her father's shirt strained against his muscles. He was a man who could easily be mistaken for an immortal god, with his fierce nature and strong sensuality.

Clearly, her brain was turning soft.

But as he ate, he used his hands to pick up the food, not touching the fork she'd placed beside his plate. He drank the ale she'd given him and seemed pleased by the meal. Juliana finished her food and stood from the table, helping Grelod clear the dishes away.

"Will you show me where I am to sleep?" he asked.

"I thought Grelod..." Her words trailed away when she suddenly realized that this was his way of wanting to talk with her again.

"I'll put Harry to bed," her maid offered. The old woman gathered up a large quilt and handed it to Juliana.

Though she accepted the quilt, her heart began quaking within her. She led the man outside, and her breath formed clouds in the air. It had grown dark, and she shivered in the cold.

The tiny shelter was barely large enough for two horses, let alone this man. Still, she brought him inside, searching for a place where he could sleep.

Guilt filled her up inside, for the interior was freezing and filthy. No man should have to sleep like this. It simply wasn't right. She faltered, not knowing what to say, when Thorgrim took her hand and led her to the back of the space. His palm was warm against her own cool flesh.

"Your servant says I may stay only until the moon completes its phases."

Words failed her, for she didn't want to believe that any of this was happening. "You don't have to stay at all. This isn't your problem, and I—"

"Do you want me to stay?" His voice was dark and deep, reaching past her inhibitions. In the darkness, she was fully aware of him. He pressed her back against the wood, his body so near, she could sense the heat of him.

Yes, I want you to stay. How she longed to lean on someone, to have him share her burden and help her overcome it. In this darkness, she was acutely aware of him. The heat of his skin allured her, making her want to rest her cheek against his chest, enclosed in his arms.

"There's nothing you can do," she said at last. "This is about proving I was legally married." She wished now that she had never taken those vows with William. At the time, she had been young and naïve, believing every word he had spoken. But after he'd gone, she had learned to rely upon herself. She had grown stronger, realizing that her husband had abandoned her. Though it had hurt her feelings, she understood that she was better off without him. A marriage in name only was better than a husband who constantly belittled her.

And yet, within a single night, she had reverted to the weak woman she had been, blindly succumbing to a man's seduction. It bothered her deeply that she'd let this stranger touch her as if she was a woman starved for affection.

"You are wrong, Juliana," Arik said. "There is a great deal I can do before the moon grows full again. The gods sent me here for that purpose."

She doubted if he could do anything at all to help. And yet...her own efforts had been unsuccessful. Was there anything to lose by letting him try? She was beginning to wonder.

"We will return to Hawthorne House at daybreak," he insisted. "I will speak to your enemies and fight on your behalf."

She half-imagined him wielding a battle-ax against the helpless butler, and the vision made her bite back a smile. "Even if we did go to Hawthorne House, the servants would turn us away."

"Let them try." He stood taller, and crossed his arms. The arrogant expression on his face was that of a man who believed he could conquer any enemy. "Or are you too afraid to fight for your son?"

It wasn't that at all. She'd tried, truly she had. But with no means of proving herself to be the viscountess, she'd lost everything. "I don't think there's anything you can do."

"You are wrong. Hundreds of men obeyed my rule in Rogaland. I went on many raids and defeated countless enemies." He spoke with such confidence, he was beginning to sway her common sense. She had already tried everything else in her power.

This man claims he's a thousand-year-old Viking. You're losing your wits if you think he can help you.

"You don't believe in magic or traveling through time," she chided. "It's not real."

"I do not know what is real anymore," he said, his

arms closing around her. "But you are real. And so is this."

His mouth drifted across her lips in the barest kiss, tempting her to open. She tasted the warm breath of his mouth, the sleek length of his tongue as he invaded her. In the darkness, every touch was intensified, and she did not know what he would do next.

"Do you deny that I am real?" His hands moved down her spine, drawing her hips to his. Against her body, she felt the length of his desire, and between her legs, she softened to it, wanting him.

"I don't know you," she whispered, as his mouth came down over her throat, his hands rising to fill with her breasts. A shuddering gasp caught in her throat as he stroked the tips, reminding her of how he'd given her such pleasure.

"But you are no maiden. And I find myself wanting to be inside you again." To illustrate his words, he slid himself against her, the hard ridge evoking the instinctive needs she couldn't deny.

"Please don't," she whispered.

"You try my patience, woman. Already you have shared my bed. Why do you resist what I know you need?" His hand moved against her gown, sliding beneath it until he was stroking her thigh.

She was wet and aching for him. If she asked it of him, she didn't doubt he would have her against the back wall, filling her up with rigid thrusts. Her breasts were tight, and when he cupped her intimately, she tightened her thighs around his hand.

"I can feel what you want, Juliana," he said, his mouth moving back to her lips. With two fingers, he entered her, and a dark moan escaped her. Gently, he tantalized her with his thick fingers, moving deep inside. She closed her eyes, unable to breathe as he coated his fingers with her essence, his thumb exerting pressure upon her hooded flesh. "Let me take you there."

Was this how a courtesan felt before taking a lover? This sense of desperate need, while her mind and body warred with one another? Her fingers dug into his shoulders, but she forced herself to back away from him.

"Don't touch me," she whispered. "I cannot forget that I am another man's wife. And I can't forget what's important right now." Slowly, she drew his hand out from beneath her skirts, struggling to catch her breath. "You may sleep on the floor within my house. But not in my bed."

She could feel the silent frustration from him, the words he would not say. He was as aroused as she was, and at the moment, he was dangerous, feral in his wild desire.

"There will come a time, Juliana of Arthur, when you will beg to share my bed." But he made no move to seize her or take her against her will.

And she feared very much that he was right.

CHAPTER FOUR

*A*rik found himself aboard a large ship, the vessel tossing upon the sea as a violent storm shredded the sails. He heard himself calling out orders to his men, in a strange language.

Juliana's language.

Such could not be possible. He knew not her words, nor could he speak them. But he gripped the mast, the rain pouring over him. He saw his men swept overboard by vicious waves, and he prayed for mercy in that language.

Lord, save me. Give me another chance to live, and bring me home.

The waves quieted, and the blood-red moon slid out from beneath a cloud. The world slipped into stillness, and he felt the breath of fear pass over him.

He thought he heard the whisper of a woman's voice on the wind. Her words summoned him, and he felt his spirit being ripped free of his body.

Arik bolted upright and found himself lying on the floor

of the house. His skin was frigid, and his mind was reeling from a tangle of thoughts he didn't understand. Images roared through him, memories that didn't belong to this life. Madness was descending upon him, and he fought it with every breath.

"Did you have a bad dream?" a boy's voice asked.

Arik glanced up and curled his hands into a fist. Once again, he'd understood the boy's words. The response came to his lips, though he hardly trusted what he was saying. "Yes. A nightmare."

The boy sat down beside him, and in the dim glow of the firelight, he saw the child smile. Harry reached out his hand and the small fingers curled against his. "It's all right. I'm here."

The gentle response was one Juliana had likely given Harry over the years, but this child's simple trust rocked him to his very soul. They were strangers, and yet the boy was offering him comfort.

He squeezed the child's hand, and the boy added, "I'm glad you're talking now. Do you want another blanket? I could give you mine."

Arik stood, still holding the boy's hand. He wanted to push back at the foreign presence within his mind that comprehended these strange words. It was like having another spirit dwelling within him. He could not know if it was a benevolent god helping him or whether it was madness drawing him under.

"Go back to sleep, boy," he said quietly, guiding the child to the small bed that pulled out from beneath his mother's. He helped the boy get under the covers and tucked him in, smoothing his hair back. Harry smiled at him, before closing his eyes.

He understood why Juliana would fight for this child. Why she would sacrifice everything to give him a better home and a better life. He would do the same, were he in her position.

Although he did not know what had summoned him across time, he believed their lives were intertwined with his.

And somehow he would save them.

Arik stared at the red stone fortress before him and it was clear why Juliana wanted it back. The structure was massive, a fortification that stood tall above the landscape with ivy curling up the side. There was no ditch to keep out invaders, nor were there guards posted—only a large gate to prevent enemies from attacking. The road led up the hillside and curved around the front of the fortress. It had taken them two days of traveling on horseback to reach it, and he was well pleased by the sight of the dwelling.

"This is Hawthorne House," she explained, still speaking in Norwegian. Arik had already decided not to tell her that he was beginning to understand her Anglo-Saxon words, for he hardly trusted the strange language. "I lived here after my marriage to William." Upon Juliana's face, he saw the wistful longing, as if she missed this place.

"Was he a king, then?" Arik guessed.

She smiled and shook her head. "No. Only a viscount, and he was never good with money. He inherited a large sum from his father and spent it as he pleased. He also traveled a great deal on the Continent." A shadow crossed her face, and she folded her hands. "He never returned, and they searched for many years before declaring his brother guardian of the lands. Marcus is now the acting viscount, according to the law, unless William returns."

"Do you want your husband to be dead?"

She crossed her arms, and tightened her cloak around her. "I don't want him to come back, if that's what you mean. But I want Harry to inherit what belongs to him. This property, along with another in London, should be entailed to him. Not Marcus, William's younger brother."

"And this…Marcus…was the one who removed you from your home."

She nodded. "He told me that he'd allowed me to stay far longer than he should have, for the sake of my son. But once the lands were declared to be under his guardianship, he ordered me to go. I think it was because he will be married soon. His wife may wish to live here."

He didn't miss the dismay upon her face. Whether or not she would admit it, Juliana missed this home. He could see it in the way she drank in her surroundings, and in the way she walked the land with a sense of ownership.

Arik kept within the trees but moved toward the outer perimeter. "Where are the servants and guards for this place?"

"There's supposed to be a land steward and a small staff, but I don't know where they are now. Until Marcus returns, most of his servants will remain with him in London."

"Then there are few people to defend it?"

Her eyes narrowed, as if she could guess his thoughts. "At the moment. But we can't simply walk in and take possession of the house. Someone would find out, and I would be guilty of trespassing." She shook her head and admitted, "I shouldn't have let you bring me here. I don't know how you talked me into it, except that I didn't know what else to do."

He ignored her doubts and continued, "If the house

rightfully belongs to your son, then it is not trespassing."

"I have no means to prove it. I'm still searching for the evidence." She followed him along the property boundaries, both of them remaining out of view from anyone who might see them. "But when I find it, I will reclaim this property for Harry."

Arik inspected the land surrounding the house, searching for any threat. There did not seem to be any outward danger, which made him even more wary. A property of this wealth would never stand unprotected.

"I am going to take a closer look," he told Juliana. "Wait here."

"But you don't have to—"

He touched a finger to her lips. "Do not fear for me." He'd gone on enough raids to recognize danger when he spied it. The house appeared abandoned from what he could see.

With a sword in his hand, he strode to the iron gates and examined them. The craftsmanship was like nothing he'd seen before, as was the lock that bound them. When he attempted to break it open with the hilt of his sword, the gates held fast. Yet, there was nothing to prevent him from climbing over them.

"Mr. Thorgrim—truly, you needn't do this."

Still she refused to call him by his name. He ignored her words, sheathing his weapon. A gnarled walnut tree rested nearby, and he climbed up, moving across the tallest branch to drop over the tall hedge that grew beside the entrance. Keeping his back to the hedge, he sniffed the air for the evidence of a hearth fire. There was nothing, save the cool winter air.

Silence hung over the property, making him more confident about entering the grounds. He continued along the path of crushed rock leading toward the house. A curved staircase led up to the doors, and he spied elaborate handles upon each. He touched one, astounded at such symmetry. He pulled the handle, but the door wouldn't budge.

With the hilt of his sword, he pounded on the wood, demanding entrance. The low thud echoed in the stillness, but no one came to the door. He kept his sword ready, listening hard for any sound, while his other hand rested upon his battle-ax. He narrowed his gaze upon the door, wondering whether he should attempt to hack at the wood with his ax, when he heard footsteps from behind him.

He spun with his sword, prepared to swing, when he saw Juliana standing a few paces away. "Wait." She hurried forward, and he saw that the gates in the distance were now open.

He sheathed the weapon. "How did you get inside?"

A guilty look passed over her. "I used the keys. I tried to tell you, but you weren't listening to me." She withdrew a narrow iron key and showed it to him. With an apologetic look, she added, "Also, I wanted to stable the horses and ensure that no one was here before I joined you. But you needn't chop the door down."

He crossed his arms over his chest while she slid a different key into the keyhole. The door unlocked, and she pressed down on the handle, pushing the door open.

The interior smelled of dust, as if no one had set foot inside the dwelling for months. "When did you leave?" he asked Juliana.

"Last summer. Marcus came and escorted me out, but I kept a key that he didn't know about." She rubbed her shoulders against the chilly interior, walking through one room, then the next. "I thought he would have been here by now, but it seems he must have had a reason to stay in London during the winter." She frowned, adding, "And it doesn't seem that the servants took very good care of Hawthorne House."

The space was dizzying in its vastness. Arik had never been inside a fortress of this size before, and as he followed her through the rooms, he saw foreign objects that he didn't recognize. With every step, he grew more wary of his environment. Uneasiness crept beneath his skin, and he gripped his battle-ax.

Juliana walked over to a tall wooden box, adjusting some weights and twisting a metal object across the numbered face. He passed by the strange object, and when a loud gong resounded from within it, he swung his ax without thinking.

The blade bit into the rectangular structure, which continued to make loud noises. He lifted his weapon, prepared to swing again, when Juliana gave a cry of alarm.

"It's a grandfather clock, Thorgrim. Nothing more." She let out a dismayed sigh as he lowered the ax.

He didn't know what a "clock" was, but the wooden structure was making a ticking sound that unnerved him. Everything, from the soft carpet beneath his feet to the elaborate textiles upon the furnishings, made him more aware that he was no longer within his own time. He knew nothing of this world, not even what was dangerous or what was safe. How could he even hope to protect Juliana when he didn't understand anything about this place?

When he had been inside Juliana's home, the interior had reminded him of his own dwelling. Simple and unadorned, with only a bed pallet and a hearth, along with a few belongings.

But this…this was too much.

His head ached, trying to absorb it all. The floor

coverings were woven in a rare pattern, likely from the lands far to the East. Silver candlesticks rested upon furnishings, and he spied a large object with a panel of white and black rectangular pieces. When he touched one, it let out a high-pitched musical sound.

He sat down in a chair, his gaze stony, while he fastened the ax at his waist. Tall glass windows let in the light, and the grim morning clouds reflected his mood.

"Are you all right?" Juliana asked.

He could give her no answer. She moved closer, studying him with concerned eyes. He could smell her skin, and the floral aroma pulled him back to her. Though he could not understand what was happening, or why he'd been brought here, he reached for her hand and gripped it.

"You're cold," she said, rubbing his hand with hers. "Are you not feeling well?"

"I've never seen a place such as this," he admitted. "With objects that make noises and wealth greater than a king's."

She stared at him, and likely she believed he'd gone soft in the head. She couldn't accept that a soul could travel across time. Nor had he truly believed it until now, when he was faced with so many unusual objects.

He drew Juliana between his knees, just holding her hands. She was his anchor to the world, steadying him through this terrible dream.

"Perhaps we should return to my father's house," she suggested.

Inwardly, he wanted to, but that was a coward's path. He couldn't allow his own fears to dominate what must be done. "Not yet. Show me the rest."

She led him through a labyrinth of rooms, and as they walked, he noticed her graceful movement and the way she held herself like a queen. This was why the gods had brought him to her. Juliana of Arthur had fallen from her throne, and her son would be heir to these lands.

But there was one door she did not open. She started to turn around, but he paused. "What lies inside that chamber?"

"My husband's room," she admitted. "It has a connecting door to mine, but I see no reason to go inside." There was a darkness upon her face, the look of a woman who had experienced pain. Without asking for her permission, Arik approached the door and opened it.

The interior smelled as if it had not been aired out in years, and a thin layer of dust covered the furnishings. Juliana followed him with reluctance. She opened one of the large window coverings, coughing as she did so.

Morning sunlight spilled into the room. A large bed stood in the center, carved of wood with four posts rising toward the ceiling and a canopy. The floor was covered with a softer woven carpet, and he bent to touch it with his hands.

She indulged him, though he could tell she wanted to be out of this room immediately. Color flushed upon her face, and she remained over by the window, far away from the bed. Arik stood and went to touch one of the wooden posts. It was beautifully carved, with grooves etched in the wood and the image of leaves near the base. The bed covering, though dusty, was soft and warm. He sat upon the mattress, his weight sinking it down, and he imagined what it would be like to sleep in such luxury. His own home boasted little more than a pallet upon the floor, though he'd had dreams of one day owning a bed like this.

"You've seen his room," Juliana said, starting to close

the window coverings. "I think we should go back. Someone might find us and—"

"You said you did not share his room. Why?" If Juliana had been his bride, they would share a room and only one bed. He couldn't fathom why a husband might send his wife to sleep elsewhere. It was unnatural.

"William did not believe it was proper." Her face turned crimson, and she started toward the door. "He visited me in my room, and sometimes he ordered me to come to his. I left afterward."

"Did he hurt you?" Arik saw her stiffen as her hand reached the door.

"N-no."

"I don't believe you." He remained on the bed, watching the excuses form upon her lips.

"I obeyed him, as a good wife should." She kept her back turned, and he suspected she didn't want to reveal the emotions she was holding back. Most of the happily married women he'd known had smiled and blushed at the mention of joining with their husbands. But not Juliana.

"Come here," he murmured.

"I don't want to."

"Do I frighten you?"

She shook her head, but remained standing in place. "I don't like this room, Thorgrim. It bothers me."

Upon her face, he saw her fear, and he didn't doubt that her husband had misused her. A sense of anger curled inside him, for it was wrong to harm a woman. If Juliana were his, she would never experience anything except her own pleasure.

Desire tightened within him as he remembered how she'd arched beneath him, taking his body. It had been a reckless claiming, one that haunted him still. He wanted to touch her again, to watch her achieve her own release as he sheathed himself inside her body—the way she had that night on the ship.

The old woman's warning, that he had less than a month to help Juliana, was a strong reminder that it was not wise to form ties with this world. Or with this woman. And yet, he wanted to take away her sadness in a way that both of them would enjoy.

He lay back upon the mattress, sinking into a softness he'd never experienced before. "I like this bed."

"We're not staying here," she warned.

He stretched out his arms, folding them under his head. "I could sleep very well on a bed such as this."

"I'm sorry, but you can't. Not on his bed."

There it was. That frowning look, as if she was thinking of what she'd lost instead of enjoying the moment. He grew weary of her protests and stood. The moment he lifted her off the ground, she began to protest, until he flung her upon the bed.

"What are you doing?"

"You should try this." He pulled her to lie beside him. "A man could enjoy a…a bed like this one, with a woman at his side. It is like nothing I have known before."

Her cheeks had gone pink, and when she lay beside him, he traced a finger over her face. When he moved his hand to her throat, he felt the wild pulse beneath his fingers. "Imagine yourself beneath this coverlet, wearing nothing at all."

She started to sit up, but he caught her hand. "Would you not rather make another memory upon this bed?"

Juliana went motionless, and she would not look at him. "That isn't the sort of woman I am."

He pressed her back, brushing his mouth against her cheek. With his fingers splayed above her breast, he murmured against her throat, "You enjoyed that night. You wanted me."

"I don't deny it. But I thought you were a dream. I never imagined—" Her words broke off when he reached to the back of her gown, where several round, hard objects clasped the fabric together. He pulled at the edges, trying to free her from the garment.

She took one of the pillows and whacked him with it. "Keep your hands to yourself, Thorgrim."

He stared at her in disbelief. She'd actually struck him? A white feather descended from the pillow, and he grinned, contemplating his next move. He picked up another pillow and held it like a shield.

A strange smile crossed her face. "Don't you dare." In warning, she picked up her own pillow.

But the moment he lowered his guard, Juliana struck him hard across the cheek, releasing a flurry of white feathers. Then she sent him a sly smile, revealing her own sense of mischief.

It was the last thing he'd expected. It seemed that Juliana of Arthur had more daring than he'd imagined.

"You struck me, woman. For that, I will retaliate." Without mercy, he whacked her shoulder with the pillow.

A laugh broke free from her, and she began striking him back until the feathers fell like snowflakes. He had never seen her like this, no longer filled with melancholy but instead playful. He wanted Juliana to smile like this all the time.

"I think we've butchered these pillows," she said. "When Marcus returns to this room, he will be quite surprised to see what we've done." She reached out and plucked a feather from his hair, and he caught her wrist.

"I like hearing you laugh." He kept his grip light, stroking her skin with his thumb. He fixed his gaze upon her, not bothering to conceal his desire. She was a beautiful woman, and he intended to touch her again.

He took her by the shoulders and lowered her back to the bed. Without asking permission, he reached back to the fastenings of her gown, wanting his mouth upon her bare skin.

"You cannot have me," she responded.

"Can I not?" He lowered his mouth to the soft space between her shoulder and throat. The moment he kissed her, she let out a shuddering breath.

"I fight for what I want, Juliana. And I never give up." He threaded his hand through her hair, bringing his mouth to the space above her bosom. "If I have to kill the man who took these lands from you, then I will. If my life's blood spills, then I shall at last have my immortality in Valhalla."

He cut off her words of protest by kissing her. Her lips were sweet, like a summer plum. He tasted her, prompting her to open her mouth for him. She was yielding to him, kissing him back as he gave up on the gown and moved his hands to her skirts. Here, at least, he could touch her.

"I did not know who you were on the night I claimed you," he said, lowering his mouth to her calf. "I thought you were the woman who betrayed me." He kissed the back of her knee and was rewarded with her cry and the outbreak of gooseflesh upon her skin. When she didn't push him away, he knew that she was enjoying his touch. It suddenly made his seduction more interesting because she was nearly clothed.

"I didn't know what I was doing," she murmured. "I thought you were a dream." A gasp broke forth when he cupped her intimately, feeling the wetness of her arousal against his palm. "Mr. Thorgrim, you mustn't."

But her body didn't lie about what she was feeling. "My name is Arik." He stroked her, capturing her mouth in a kiss that was meant to silence her dismay.

Her busy mind was working again, making her believe she should not take pleasure with him. His own lust was raging, but this time, she didn't kiss him back.

"I don't know if my husband is alive or dead, Thorgrim," she said against his mouth. And then he realized that her sense of honor was holding her back. Unlike Svala, she would not betray the man she was bound to. She had not willingly shared herself that night—she'd believed he wasn't real.

And for that reason, he stopped immediately. His body ached with physical desire, but it was a punishment he deserved.

Any of your kinsmen would simply take her, his mind taunted. *They would not ask for her consent.*

Arik had the strength to overpower her, and though his tribe was not known for mercy, he would never take a woman against her will. He preferred a yielding female body clenched around him, as she arched with a rush of release. That was far better than a woman who fought back.

He didn't argue when she got off the bed and walked toward the window. Juliana pressed her hand against the flat pane of glass, her mood somber once again. She looked as if she was berating herself for the moment with him.

He swung his legs over the side of the bed and walked toward her. "Did you love your husband?"

She held her ground but didn't look at him. "I thought I did when I married him. But I loved a man who did not exist."

"Then you should put aside the marriage and find a

man who is more deserving of you." Even if it could never be him, he did not believe Juliana should grieve for an unworthy man.

He pressed his palm to the glass, feeling its strange cool texture. It was a marvel to him that anyone could make something as hard as stone that a person could see through. He had seen glass before during his voyages, but never had it been this transparent. It was yet another reminder of how vast the years were between them.

From this view, the green meadows spread for miles, while evergreen pines dotted the base of the hills. There was a familiarity to this land, a sense that he had seen this place before. And when he glimpsed a lone pillar of rock at the top of the highest hill, a chill slid through his veins.

"I know this place," he said to Juliana. "My brother held these lands."

Magnus had traveled and settled here, more than a thousand years ago. He remembered the settlement, for his brother had created his dwelling at the top of the highest point while other longhouses encircled it. They had chosen a place where they could easily see their enemies approaching, both on land and by sea.

A coldness centered within him, with the sense that the gods were reweaving his destiny once again. It could not be a coincidence that he had been brought to this place.

Juliana frowned as she studied the standing stone in the distance. "Those lands belong to Gregory Fielding, the Duke of Somerford."

"Do you know him?"

She shrugged. "We've met a time or two."

Abruptly, she frowned, catching his hand. She studied the outline of his face, her gaze sharpening with uncertainty. "*That's* where I know you. You remind me of the duke's son." She stared at him as if she believed he was someone else. "His name is Eric, too. His courtesy title is the Marquess of Thorgraham."

The names were similar, and it unnerved him as he remembered the dream where he had seen visions that were not his own. *Whose memories did you see in your dream?* the voice of reason insisted. *How can you speak a language that is not yours?*

Juliana had gone deathly pale. "The duke's son was lost at sea, years ago." She reached out to touch his face, studying him. "Is that who you truly are? I know that sometimes men who are wounded can suffer from losing their memories."

"No," he answered. "I am the son of Valdr, not Gregory." Any similarity between them was merely a twist of fate, nothing more.

It was as if his spirit had crossed paths with another, switching places. He could not deny that he'd remembered visions that were not his. But it could easily have been tricks played by the gods.

He could not think of that now. It was better to concentrate on the task at hand, on how to win back this woman's lands. That was the reason why he'd been sent here, and he had to believe that defeating her enemies would win him the honor he needed to reach Valhalla.

But he did want to visit the ruins of his brother's longhouse. Magnus had placed the stone at the center of his settlement, and Arik wondered if the runes would reveal any missing pieces of the past.

"We must go to my brother's settlement," Arik insisted. He was certain that this was somehow a part of his purpose. Of all the places the gods could have sent him, why else would he be back at his brother's longhouse?

"Now?" Juliana questioned. "But we cannot simply trespass on the duke's lands. His Grace may not be receiving visitors."

Arik ignored her misgivings and answered, "First, we will go there." He pointed toward the stone monolith.

"Why?"

"We will find answers there," he said. "Possibly my brother's hoard of gold, if we are fortunate. You may wish to find a digging tool." If he did find the hoard, they could use it to hire mercenaries. Despite the thousand years that had passed, the promise of wealth was a timeless offering to any man.

Arik opened the door and began striding toward the stairs while Juliana hurried behind him. "We cannot trespass upon the duke's land, much less dig holes there," she insisted. "It isn't right."

He dismissed her protests, certain that this was where he needed to be. "We'll get our horses first. You said they were in the stables?"

"Yes, but—"

"Good. We leave now." He allowed her to shut the door behind them, and she muttered something about his stubbornness.

She would soon change her mind, if his brother had indeed left behind a hoard of gold and treasure. Such wealth would give Juliana a very different sort of power, one she desperately needed.

It was becoming painfully obvious that Arik Thorgrim believed he was a Viking. A very stubborn, bull-headed Viking who wouldn't listen to reason, no matter what she told him. She didn't believe his tale of traveling through time, and undoubtedly she ought to be more than a little afraid of him. It was madness that she'd brought him to Hawthorne House.

But...beneath his arrogant confidence, she suspected that he *would* try to help her son. He had been patient and kind to Harry, and when they'd said farewell, the boy had hugged him. It had hurt to see them together, as if Mr. Thorgrim were the sort of man who could be a father to Harry.

No. If he wanted to help them, that was all right, but he could never stay. It wasn't good for either of them.

They continued riding toward the stone monolith, and Juliana prayed that none of the duke's servants would see them. Otherwise, she would have to invent a reason why they'd come.

Mr. Thorgrim hardly cared that they were trespassing. Moreover, he'd brought a shovel with him and two empty feed sacks. Why in the world would he believe a treasure was buried near the stone monolith? Even if there was, surely thieves would have found it by now. But her protests had fallen upon deaf ears. He simply sent her a look as if he didn't have to explain himself.

Once they reached the standing stone, he dismounted and helped her down. He tethered the horses to let them graze and then walked over to the monolith.

"Do you recognize it?" she asked.

Thorgrim nodded. He ran his hands over the rough granite, as if searching for something. She did the same but could see nothing. "What are you looking for?" The gray stone had worn and weathered over time, and rose several inches above her in height.

"My brother carved runes upon this stone. Sometimes he marked the location of his hoard, using markings only his family would understand. But they are gone now." He ran his hands over the surface, and the expression on his face was uneasy. "I wonder if the wind and rains wore them off the stone over these thousand years."

A cold breeze swept over her nape, and Juliana sensed his disquiet. She didn't believe that he had crossed through time. He couldn't possibly be a Viking. And yet, her maid Grelod's words came back to her:

"I know what you are. And I know from whence you came, Viking. I prayed to Freya on my lady's behalf, and the goddess summoned you here for her."

Superstitious rot, her brain reminded her. It could not be true.

And yet, this man knew nothing of things as simple as clocks or featherbeds. He gave her son a knife as a gift and ignored all propriety, stealing kisses from her. By every indication, he was a barbarian. An honorable one, perhaps, but rough-mannered all the same.

She shut down the thought. The most sensible explanation was that he was the duke's son, returned from the sea. Likely he had experienced such hardships, it had caused a temporary madness.

But *he* believed it with an unshakable conviction. There was no means of forcing him to face reality.

Arik continued to search, but he could find no markings whatsoever upon the stone. "It should *be* here." He drove the side of his fist into the stone as if that would bring forth the answers.

Juliana said nothing, for she didn't exactly believe in any sort of Viking hoard. She leaned back against the stone, resting upon the soft grass. It was peaceful from up here, with a view of the sea in the distance. Beside her, Arik's expression held wariness. "I know my brother. He would have hidden his hoard nearby, if there was anything left."

She gave a slight shrug, as if it didn't matter. "Do you want to go back?" Right now, she felt uncomfortable trespassing upon the duke's land.

"You do not believe me, do you? You do not believe that I am who I say I am." He stood over her, his shadow blocking out the sun.

She was about to say no, but the words wouldn't come. Juliana rubbed her arms against the chill that crept over her. She considered herself a pragmatic woman, one who didn't believe in ghosts or strange mysteries. But that night *had* held an eerie, otherworldly quality. "I don't know what to believe."

And that was the truth. There were no explanations for the way she'd been carried off to sea or rescued by a man who claimed he was from a thousand years earlier. It had seemed real enough on that night—far too real.

When she glanced over at him, his expression held frustration. Despite what he'd claimed, there were no markings upon the standing stone.

She felt sympathetic toward him, for an unknown reason. He appeared angry and frustrated, a man who had lost everything. Whether or not Arik Thorgrim could do anything to help her prove Harry's legitimacy, he *was* trying. And madman or not, he was the only one who had stood by her.

Juliana tried not to look at him, but she was well aware of the caged strength in his arms. There was a wildness about him, the sense that this man could never be tamed. And she found herself wanting to help him, as foolish as it might be.

There is no such thing as a Viking hoard buried here, her sensible side insisted. *You're being ridiculous.*

And yes, she was, but was there any harm in

searching? If nothing else, it might convince Arik that he was mistaken.

Juliana ran her hands along the base and saw that the grass completely covered it on all sides. The dirt was hardened around the stone, but it seemed that the monolith was buried several feet down. She reached for the shovel and tried to push back some of the dirt. When she stepped upon the tool, the grass was too thick for the shovel blade to sink through.

"What are you trying to do?" he asked, reaching for the handle.

She let him have the shovel and offered, "If there is any sort of marking upon this stone, it might have been deliberately covered up. Or perhaps it sank into the ground over time. We should dig around the stone and see if there are any markings lower in the earth."

A flare of interest sparked in his eyes. "I had not thought of such. You may be right."

Abruptly, he set the shovel against the stone and seized her face between his hands, kissing her roughly. The unexpected affection caught her unawares, but she rather wanted to kiss him back. Before she could decide what to do, he released her.

Her pulse pounded, and it took a moment to steady herself. This man's effect upon her was far too strong— and that was dangerous.

"Go on, then," she bade him. "See if you find anything."

For the next hour, he dug all around the stone, and it soon became clear that the granite went much deeper than she'd thought. "Do you want me to help dig for a while?" she asked.

But Arik shook his head, continuing to dig until he'd gone three feet deeper. At last he set the shovel aside and rubbed at the granite. Juliana moved in closer and saw that there were indeed engraved markings, runes that made no sense to her.

The sudden look of satisfaction on his face revealed that he'd found what he was searching for.

"Can you read those?"

He traced his fingers over the carved lines and let out a slow breath, nodding.

He might be a Viking, if he could read the runes, her mind reasoned.

She didn't know what to believe. The fact that he spoke Norwegian instead of English was unusual, but then again, she had learned the language from Grelod when she was a young girl. It meant nothing.

But no one could read runes.

She closed her eyes, trying not to think of what that meant. Arik stood, his gaze fixed upon the distance. There was no triumph in his expression, but instead she saw his melancholy.

"What is it?" she asked, coming to stand beside him. "Is something wrong?"

"I was thinking of my brother," he answered quietly. "I realized that I will not see Magnus again in this lifetime."

Without knowing why, Juliana took his hand and held it. "But you will see him again in the afterlife." Once more, a chill crept over her. She sensed that these moments with Arik Thorgrim were fleeting, regardless of where he'd come from. And beneath it all was the premonition that he would die.

Which was foolish. She tried to shake away the errant thought, but the coldness remained, twining around her good sense.

"I hope I will see him again in Valhalla." He squeezed

her hand and took the shovel, walking downhill. "Come. We will leave our horses here."

"Where are we going?"

"To the stream." He led the way, but Juliana held back. The stream was closer to the duke's house, and if they ventured that far, they could be found.

"Mr. Thorgrim, we might be seen by the duke or his servants. We should not be trespassing, for these lands belong to him."

"They belong to my brother," he corrected in a cool voice. "And to *my* family. If this man wants to claim anything, let him try to take it from me."

And with that, he left her with no choice except to follow.

ৎ

Arik dug beside the streambed until the sun rimmed the horizon. His arms were covered in mud, and his fingers were wrinkled from being submerged. Yet, he felt confident that the hoard would be here.

When they were boys, he and his brother had pretended to be raiders burying their treasure. Magnus had invented a name for himself, Odinum, after the Allfather god. In their imagination, Odinum was a powerful invader, one with immense treasure. They had buried stones within the river, pretending they were ingots of gold and silver.

Upon the runestone, Arik had seen his own name, followed by the name Odinum. Though he could not know why Magnus had inscribed the name, he suspected that his brother had left an offering for him, but the river had evolved over time into a stream. He'd dug on both sides, but so far had come up with nothing. If there had been anything, it might be gone after all these years. Or buried so deeply that no man could find it.

"It's getting dark, Mr. Thorgrim. We should go back," Juliana urged.

Arik rinsed his arms off in the cold stream and regarded her. He didn't want to leave at this moment, for there was still an hour of light remaining. If there was any chance of finding a treasure for Juliana, he wanted to try. Then, too, he couldn't allow her to ride off alone.

"At sundown, I will take you back," he promised.

"Are you certain you're digging in the right place?" she asked.

"I am." His hands touched a large flat stone beneath the water, and he struggled to pry it up. A moment later, his fingers touched something cold and metallic. He dug deeper and pulled hard to bring up a lead box.

"Bring the sacks," he ordered Juliana. "We've found my brother's hoard."

They worked until the light was nearly gone, washing the lead box until he could open the lid. Inside were silver pieces, silver coins, gold, and several armbands. Juliana was as excited as he was, and she exclaimed over the intricate metal clasps. In all, he guessed there were fifty silver coins, seven armbands, and various ingots of gold.

When it was all placed inside the sack, she sobered. "I don't know what to believe about this. I know you said you were a Viking sent through time. It's madness to consider such a thing." She rested her hands in her lap, studying him. "But...I'm almost afraid it's real. You could not have found this unless you truly did read those runes."

Though it shouldn't matter whether or not she believed him, he wanted her to know that he had not lied. "I cannot guess why I was sent here, Juliana of Arthur. But I believe that we were meant to find Magnus's hoard. And my brother's gold will help to save your son." With it, he could hire the mercenaries he needed to help him on this quest.

He stood, reaching to help her up, and in the soft light of the moon, she appeared somber. "I don't know what we should do now."

Arik gripped her hand and then slid his arm around her waist. "We return to your house and make our plans."

It brought him comfort to know that his brother had indeed walked these lands. The runes had revealed not only the location of the hoard, but also the names of his brother's sons. Magnus had enjoyed a long life, and for that, Arik was grateful.

The flare of a torch caught his attention, and instantly, Arik seized his sword hilt. When he spied a man approaching on horseback, flanked by three other men, he set down the sacks containing the hoard of treasure.

But the moment he saw the man's features, his blood ran cold. Although his gray hair was shorter and he wore no beard, this man was the image of his father, Valdr.

Images and memories slammed through him, and he sensed the presence of another soul within him. *Father,* the voice within was crying out, in a language that was not his.

Arik couldn't move or speak. He was beginning to sense that his life had been traded for another's. Dreams flooded his mind, of learning to ride a horse while this man held the reins. Of listening to stories at night, before a father pulled the covers over him.

He remembered arguing about freedom and his desire

to fight. He'd left this place and this man and had nearly died at sea.

And now the man was standing before him.

His own memories and the stranger's memories intersected, each clouding the other. He had never met this man…and yet, he knew who the stranger was.

Arik took a step forward, and Juliana held her ground. "It's the duke," she whispered. "We have to leave. W— we shouldn't be here."

He shook his head. The man looked too much like the father he hadn't seen in three years. The overwhelming desire came over him, to embrace the man, though he knew it could not be his father.

"Eric?" the man murmured, holding up a torch. "Is that you?" His face had turned ashen, as if he'd never expected to see his son again. He spoke the Anglo-Saxon tongue, and each word was clear.

"He thinks you are his son," Juliana whispered in Norwegian. "The one who drowned at sea, years ago."

Arik stared at the man, not knowing what to say. He could not relinquish the belief that this man was somehow connected to his lost father. Even the name of his son was similar to his own.

He'd believed that he was sent here to help Juliana of Arthur. Now, he was beginning to wonder if there was a greater purpose for him. He stepped nearer to the man and replied, "I am Arik Thorgrim. Not your son."

Juliana's mouth dropped open when he spoke her language. A moment later, a fierce anger stole over those stormy gray eyes.

"Forgive me," the duke said. "But…you look so much like him."

The broken pieces were starting to come together. Perhaps his memories were tangled with the memories of this man's son. Perhaps they had both crossed through time during the storm. There was no way to know for certain.

"This is Gregory Fielding, His Grace the Duke of Somerford," Juliana said. He detected the note of unrest in her voice and didn't know if it was anger or fear.

The duke dismounted from his horse and approached. "Did the sea bring you here?"

Arik inclined his head. "It did."

Juliana caught his arm, her expression furious again. He knew she would want an explanation about why he was now speaking her language. But from the wrath in her eyes, she might not believe the truth.

Arik took a breath and opened the sack at his feet. Then he unfolded another sack he'd brought with him and filled it with half of his brother's hoard. He couldn't say what provoked him to give the treasure to this man, but the duke resembled his father so strongly, the urge was impossible to deny.

Then he held out the sack. "I give you half of this hoard freely. It belonged to my brother." He made no mention of where he had found the hoard, for the man might believe he had a right to it. "The rest I am giving over to Juliana's son, since his lands were stolen from him."

The duke paled, examining the contents for a moment before accepting the sack. "Come to my house in the morning. There is a great deal I should like to discuss with you."

Arik agreed with that. But even more, he wanted to better understand the connection between the strange visions and this man. "This I will do."

It almost felt as if he should go with this man now, so strong was the instinct to follow him. The look in the man's eyes reminded him so strongly of Valdr, it was all Arik could do to turn away. He guided Juliana back to their horses, still carrying half his brother's hoard in the sack. Though he helped her onto her mare, her silence was damning.

Once they were back upon her husband's lands, she drew her horse to a stop. "I cannot conceive of how I almost believed your tales. I must have been dreaming to even imagine it. I don't know if you're the duke's bastard son or—or someone Marcus paid...but you are *not* a Viking."

"I have told you who I am. Arik Thorgrim, son of Valdr."

Her face held a blend of anger and frustration. "This was such a mistake. I never should have come here with you. You've done nothing but tell lies, and I was too eager to hear them." She started to ride away, but he quickened his pace and caught up, taking her horse's reins.

"You will go nowhere, woman. We have not finished talking."

"Talking? In which language?" She swung down and began walking toward the grounds. "Norwegian? Or the English language that you supposedly couldn't speak."

"I could not speak your tongue, until the dream." He strode alongside her, catching her arm. "One morning, I awakened with knowledge of your manner of speaking, and while there are some words I do not know, more has become clear."

"Lies!" she exploded. "Now take your hands off me." Her rage was so great, her gloved hands were trembling. "I went along with this, because I know something happened that night. Something I cannot explain. But I will not stay with a man who has told falsehoods, nor will

I let him endanger my son. We were well enough without you, so you can take your Viking hoard—or whatever you want to call it—and go!"

He trusted not the English words he'd used with her, and clearly her anger had not diminished. Best to simply take her back to the house and let her eat and rest.

"I am going nowhere, Juliana of Arthur. And you lost the wager, if you will recall."

She jerked her arm away and continued walking toward the house. "Our wager is finished. If you want somewhere to stay this night, go and speak with the Duke of Somerford. I suppose the pair of you have a great deal you could talk about."

Arik wasn't going to let her go that easily. "I have more that I wish to discuss with you." He started to guide her toward the house, but she refused to take another step.

"Not in the house. Someone has returned," she told him, pointing toward the illuminated windows.

"Then we will talk here." Without asking, he lifted her up and brought her toward a wooden structure not far from the gardens.

"Put me down," Juliana insisted, squirming to get free. She weighed nearly nothing, and he ignored her protests as he opened the door. Inside, he found all manner of tools for tending the soil.

"Now we will talk with no one to interrupt," he said, setting her down near a large sack. Arik leaned against the door, blocking her from leaving. "Why do you believe that I lied to you?"

"Because men do not simply wake up and know another language! You knew it all along, and you led me to believe that you wanted to help me and my son." She lowered her tone, shaking her head. "I should have known that the only reason you brought me here was because it was close to the buried hoard. Perhaps you stole it and reburied it there." She lifted her hands in a shrug. "Not that it matters, because in the morning, I am going back to my son."

Arik paused, trying to choose the right words to say. He used his own language, trusting those words more. "The first night we met, you gave yourself to me. Why?"

Her face burned crimson. "None of that matters. It was a mistake, just as every moment with you has been wrong."

He remained on the far side of the room, speaking calmly. "It was because we were both spellbound. I believed I was with the woman I had been betrothed to. While you believed you were dreaming."

"Yes," she admitted. "I couldn't imagine you were real. And whoever you truly are, I want you to stay away from me and my son."

"Because you believe I have told you untruths." He moved in, holding her waist with both palms. She was so slender, like a willow. Her hands moved to try and push him away, but she was no match for his strength.

"I know you have." Her voice had grown quiet now, and she ceased her struggles. He softened his hold in response.

"Juliana of Arthur, as I have told you, the gods sent me here for reasons I cannot name. I do not know why my dream showed me the memories of a man whose father I met only an hour ago. Or why I can speak a language that is not my own. But this I swear to you—I will never hurt you or your son. I will guard you both and slay whatever enemies threaten you."

He lifted her chin with one palm. "Has no man ever fought for you, *kjære*?" He touched the pulse at her neck. Her heart was beating rapidly, and her cheeks were flushed. Whether it was fear or desire, he could not know.

She shook her head in silence. "I cannot believe what you say. None of it is true."

"You remember that night," he whispered darkly. "It haunts you. The way it haunts me."

She tried to break free of him, but he held her fast. "You know that we were brought together somehow. I brought you swiftly to your pleasure, and you cried out for me."

"Don't," she warned him.

He released her, and she pushed open the door, walking back toward the house. She gripped her skirts, hurrying as fast as she dared. It seemed that she intended to confront whoever was inside the house and beg shelter for the night.

"I was summoned to you," he reminded her, keeping up with her pace. "And I *will* find out why."

She stopped suddenly and spun to face him. "Do as you wish, Mr. Thorgrim. But stay away from me."

He had no intention of doing so. Yet, before she could break free of him again, he heard an older woman call out from near the house, "Juliana, is that you? Come here, girl."

Juliana had gone utterly motionless. "How on earth did she find me?" From the fear on her face, Arik suspected it was an unwanted visitor.

He leaned in, muttering, "Do I need to kill this woman?"

"You may want to, before she leaves. But no, it's only my grandmother."

CHAPTER FIVE

N ow then," Olivia Pickford, the Baroness of
Traveston, crossed her arms and regarded
Juliana. Behind the woman stood her maid and a
footman. "Juliana, would you care to explain why you are
skulking around the gardens with this man? What have
you to say for yourself?"

Words failed her, and Juliana had no idea what to say
to her grandmother. If she admitted that she had been
traveling with Arik, her grandmother would believe she
was little better than a common trollop.

Instead, she straightened and faced down the woman,
braving a smile. "It's good to see you, Grandmama. Are
you planning to stay the night at Hawthorne House?"
Stalling her was the best way to avoid answering
questions, she decided.

"Well, I wasn't about to spend the night in that hovel
your father gave you." The baroness shuddered at the
thought. "It's hardly fit for anyone." Her gaze passed over
Arik, and she pressed her lips together. "Who are you,
young man, and what, pray tell, are you doing with my
granddaughter?"

Don't answer her, Juliana wanted to plead. She had no

idea what sort of tale Mr. Thorgrim would spin, and she dreaded his answer.

But he stepped forward, regarding her grandmother. He crossed his arms and stared at her as if trying to decide what to say.

"Wait a moment," Lady Traveston interrupted, before he could utter a word. "I *do* know who you are. Your father's lands adjoin these, don't they? You're the Duke of Somerford's son."

Before Arik could answer, the baroness smiled as if she'd suddenly put the pieces together. "Lord Thorgraham, I believe. I suppose you are out walking with my granddaughter, is that it?"

"I did go walking with her, yes."

Juliana breathed a sigh of relief that he hadn't told her grandmother any strange stories. There were problems enough with the arrival of Lady Traveston. She didn't want to make matters worse.

"We all believed you'd drowned at sea." Her grandmother stepped forward, peering closer. "Your father must have been delighted at your return."

When he glanced at her, Juliana nodded. *Yes, lie. Tell her what she wants to hear.*

"I only saw him today," Arik answered. It was strange to hear him speaking English. His voice was stilted, as if he didn't trust what he was saying.

He is not who he says he is, she reminded herself. But regardless of his identity, the fact remained that she had allowed him to seduce her. And whether he was the duke's lost son or a bastard son who resembled him, she had to maintain her distance.

She had only seen the true Lord Thorgraham once, when she and her husband had attended a party at the duke's house. But William had prevented her from speaking to anyone there. He'd tried to hide her, as if she embarrassed him. And shortly afterward, she'd become pregnant with Harry and had gone into seclusion. There was no way to tell who this man really was.

"Hmm," her grandmother remarked. "Well, Lord Thorgraham, I am glad to hear that you survived your misfortunes at sea." The baroness eyed him as if she could not understand why he had not changed his clothing. Although Juliana had offered Arik more of her father's clothing, he had returned to his own garments after they had dried.

"I suppose you'll want to return home to your father to…refresh yourself," Lady Traveston continued.

"Later," he said. "Tonight I will share a meal with Juliana." His eyes fixed upon her in a silent reminder that he would not leave her side.

Wonderful. That was all she needed—Lady Traveston dining with a man who believed he was a Viking. It was nothing short of a disaster waiting to happen.

"Juliana, is it? My, have we forgotten our manners?" Her grandmother's reproach meant nothing to Thorgrim, who didn't realize that it was improper to call a lady by her first name. "In any event, are you certain you wish to dine with us instead of His Grace?" Her narrowed gaze fixed upon him again, as if she couldn't imagine why he was here.

"I made your granddaughter a promise," Arik insisted, refusing to let the baroness badger him. "And she will procure food for us."

Was he expecting her to cook? Juliana raised an eyebrow at that. He needed to understand that she wasn't even supposed to be here.

"Grandmama, why don't you walk ahead for a moment and have the servants put your belongings away in one of the bedchambers? Lord Thorgraham and I will join you momentarily."

Or at least, they would, if the servants didn't throw them out. Juliana didn't doubt for a moment that the butler would turn them away. And then what could she do? Bring her grandmother back to her father's house on a two-day journey? She'd never hear the end of it.

"I will not be dismissed just yet, Juliana. You require a chaperone, might I remind you?" The old woman squared her shoulders as if preparing for battle. "To be alone with a gentleman is—"

"I am a married woman, and there is no harm in it," she countered, sending her grandmother a dark look. The baroness looked as if she wanted to argue further but thankfully let the point go.

"No more than a few minutes," she warned. "Lord Thorgraham, I am eager to hear the story of how you managed to escape the perils of drowning."

There was entirely too much zest in her grandmother's voice, and Juliana had a feeling that she would need a glass of wine with dinner. Perhaps two, if she wanted to get through it without offending the baroness.

Lady Traveston swept her skirts aside and marched ahead of them. Juliana waited until she was out of earshot and then turned to Mr. Thorgrim.

"No matter what happens, do not mention Vikings to my grandmother," Juliana whispered. "She will think you've lost your wits."

"You still do not believe me," he said, crossing his arms again. "Why do you deny what you have seen with your own eyes?"

"Because it's impossible. *You* are impossible, and it's far more likely that you are the duke's son and you lost your memories when you were out at sea."

"The man resembles my father. But it is not he. Nor am I his son."

She didn't know what to think, but it was clear that she had to send him away. He could not seem to grasp how far-fetched his story was, and she worried that he might have a touch of madness.

"We will dine tonight," she said quietly. "And after that, you must leave." She had been so foolish to believe this man, and she could only blame her own naïveté. The truth was, she'd wanted to lean on someone, to accept help when they were struggling through this winter. And perhaps it had been her loneliness as well.

"Think you that I enjoy having my life ripped apart in this way?" he asked angrily. "That I wanted to be taken from my own time and placed in a world where nothing is as it was?" He moved in, keeping his voice low. "If I leave, I have nowhere else to go, woman. My family and friends are dead."

He was staring at her with blazing rage, and she was entirely at his mercy. His dark hair hung around his shoulders, while a white scar edged his throat. And oh, he was infuriated when his arm slid around her waist.

"I have nothing at all," he murmured. "Nothing, save you." At that, his mouth came down upon hers.

The fierce kiss was made of heated breath and half-remembered longing. She wanted to pull away, but he commanded her lips, tempting her to kiss him back. His rough mouth took possession of hers, claiming her until she could scarcely breathe. The primal yearning made her ache to be in his arms again, and she trembled with the force of the way he made her feel.

Without warning, Arik lifted her hips, fitting her body to his. She couldn't move away, even if she'd wanted to.

But he knew how to coax a response, taking her under,

until there was nothing but this man and forbidden feelings that had lain dormant for many nights. He kissed her until her lips were swollen, until her body ached with the need to be touched.

"Tell me that this is not real," he ordered, bringing his mouth to the column of her throat. "Tell me that you do not want me."

Dear God, she did. She could imagine him taking her upon the ground, his body moving inside hers. The vision brought a surge of desire, a tight aching and a dampness between her legs that revealed a hidden longing.

"I don't know who you are," she managed. "And I don't know what you want from me."

He stared at her with stony eyes before he lowered her to the ground. "I am who I said I am. And whether or not you ever believe that, know that I will bring back your son's birthright. After that, I will be gone from your life."

Her knees were barely able to support her weight, but she managed to straighten. "You cannot help me, Mr. Thorgrim. Or Lord Thorgraham—whoever you are."

"I can. And I will," he said, before he took her hand and led her back to the house.

The baroness was waiting at the front door, her arms folded across her chest. "Juliana, will you please tell this mule-headed peasant that he has no right to throw me out?"

The butler, Owen Newcastle, was blocking the doorway, looking for all the world as if he wanted to die of embarrassment. He bowed slightly. "My lady. I am sorry, but—"

"Oh, come, now," her grandmother interrupted. "I

have traveled many miles to see my granddaughter, Mr. Newcastle. You *do* remember me, don't you?"

"Lady Traveston, of course."

Juliana knew exactly what Newcastle thought of Lady Traveston, and she was not among his favorite guests. His polite smile was starting to falter.

"And you do *not* intend to turn a baroness and her servants away when she has journeyed this far, I am quite certain." The blistering look she sent toward the butler was undeniable. It was as if she was daring him to make a spectacle.

Which Mr. Newcastle would never do. Her former butler was proper with a capital *P*. When he said nothing, Lady Traveston beamed at him. "Very good. I *knew* you were a dependable gentleman, and I shall see to it that you are rewarded for your service."

But then the butler's gaze turned, and he sent Juliana an apologetic look. "I have orders that Lady Hawthorne—that is, Miss Nelson—may not set foot upon the premises."

Of course Juliana had known that, but her grandmother was outraged. Lady Traveston's face turned the color of a boiled beet. "You're not serious. Just because of a *misunderstanding*, you intend to refuse hospitality to a young woman who has been mistress of your household for six years?"

Her grandmother was fully aware of the scandal surrounding Juliana's marriage, but she was facing down the butler with justified outrage. It made Juliana wonder why she had suddenly decided to intervene. Why now, after it had been six months?

You must swallow your pride and let her help you, her common sense reminded her. This was about Harry and providing for him.

The butler grimaced. "I fear I cannot give the former viscountess our hospitality. Marcus Arthur, the acting Viscount Hawthorne, has strictly forbidden it. I would lose my post if I disobeyed."

"My dear man, that is the *least* of your troubles," Lady Traveston insisted. She stepped forward, pushing her way past the threshold. "We have a caller, the Duke of Somerford's son." With a flourish of her arm, she presented him. "I believe you remember the Marquess of Thorgraham."

The butler whitened, as if he had no idea what to do at this moment. He eyed Arik with wariness. "You look…quite different, my lord."

"Yes, well, most men *do* look different when they nearly drown at sea." Lady Traveston forced the door open wider. "Now, you and the servants are going to prepare a good meal for the duke's son. Or I promise you, all of London will hear about how this gallant man was turned away from Lord Hawthorne's hospitality."

"And Miss Nelson will leave afterward?" the butler asked hopefully.

"She stays with me," Arik insisted. When he moved beside her, the threat in his bearing was unmistakable. Though Juliana supposed she ought to be slightly annoyed, it was rather nice to see the butler take a step backward.

"I—that is, I'm not certain—"

"Mr. Newcastle, honestly. Does anyone need to know that she's here?" Lady Traveston continued. "I think not. If you are truly that concerned about losing your post, I can assure you that I will tell no one of Juliana's presence. But if you turn my darling granddaughter away, I shall make your life into a living nightmare."

Never in her life had Juliana been referred to as a

darling granddaughter—more often she was *that girl.*
Even so, she understood the baroness's intentions.

"Furthermore, I expect that the servants will prepare
rooms for both my granddaughter and me. Both of us are
in need of shelter for the night, so that we may retire in
comfort. And of course, my coachman, my footman, and
my maid must have a place to stay." Lady Traveston
pointed in the direction of her coach. Then she lifted her
chin toward Newcastle, who took another step backward.
"See to it, won't you?"

"I'll see what can be done, my lady. But I do ask for
your discretion." The butler signaled for a footman to
come forward, and he leaned down to give the man
instructions.

"Of course." Lady Traveston beckoned for Juliana and
Arik to enter.

At that moment, Thorgrim sent the woman an
admiring smile. "You remind me of my own mother," he
said. "She was quite fierce, like you."

Lady Traveston flushed and cleared her throat. "I
suppose that's meant to be a compliment. But although
you may dine with Juliana and me, I do expect you to
return home afterward. To your *own* bedchamber." At
that, the older woman left them standing in the hall while
she went to explore the downstairs.

Juliana wanted to groan at the woman's insinuation.
But Arik only smiled. He wasn't thinking of sharing *her*
bed, was he? But from the look in his eyes, yes, that was
exactly what he was thinking.

She ought to send him away to beg for hospitality
from the duke. His Grace was unlikely to turn Arik away.

But he leaned in and asked, "Will I have to sleep
outside with the horses?"

"No." Juliana's voice came out like a whisper. "I will

find a place for you here." *Mistake!* her brain was screaming. *You cannot let him remain.* For in a comfortable manor house such as this, he could easily tempt her back into seduction.

"Where?" he asked. His hand brushed against hers, and she knew it was no accident.

Juliana squared her shoulders and faced him. In a low voice, she instructed, "After the meal ends, you will pretend to leave." She nodded toward the stairs a few feet away. "Go up to the third floor and open the last door on the left. It should suffice."

Without another word, she hurried forward to catch up to her grandmother. Lady Traveston strode toward the parlor with the precision of a soldier marching into battle. She paused briefly at the end of the hallway when she saw the remains of the grandfather clock. "Good heavens. Whatever happened here?"

Juliana met Arik's gaze, and for a moment, she could not speak. He had tried to slay the clock, as if it were a supernatural object. The Duke of Somerford's son would never do such a thing, no matter how much he'd forgotten. Nor would a duke's bastard. He would have known it was a clock and disregarded it.

But Arik had been affected by more than the clock. He'd stared at the pianoforte as if he'd never seen one before. And he'd touched the Oriental rugs as if they were rare and precious.

Her heartbeat quickened. Was it possible that she'd been wrong about him?

"Well?" the baroness demanded, pointing to the damaged wood.

"It was—merely an accident, Grandmama. Nothing more than that." But after they passed the grandfather clock, she took a moment to truly look at Arik Thorgrim.

He was so very tall, and she suspected he was taller than the duke's son. His face held many scars, as did his forearms. He was a warrior, not a gentleman. It was as evident as the dark brown eyes that held her captive.

Dear God, who *was* he?

"Juliana?" her grandmother prompted. "Are you going to just stand there and stare at Lord Thorgraham?"

"N-no." She moved forward into the parlor and sank down into a chair, so grateful for a moment to sit down. Dizziness swept over her, and she took slow breaths to calm her beating heart.

Lady Traveston sat down and sighed. Her girth spilled over the edges of the fragile gilt chair, but she perched upon it as if she were a queen. She gestured for Arik to sit, and when he did, she began her interrogation. "Now, I wish to hear all about the night your ship disappeared, Lord Thorgraham. Do not leave out a single detail."

He sent her a sidelong glance and then corrected, "You may call me Arik."

"It is far too soon to be on such familiar terms," her grandmother said. "But we may become friends in time." She waved her hand. "Now do tell me where you've been."

Arik told her of sailing across the sea and of the violent storm. He wove a tale of his men dying and how his ship had arrived upon the shore.

"So you were the only survivor?" Lady Traveston asked.

He nodded. "And I have sworn to help Juliana fight for her son."

At the mention of Harry, Juliana's spirits dimmed. Though she knew he was safe with Grelod, it seemed wrong to stay in this house without him.

"These lands rightfully belong to them," Arik continued. "They cannot remain in her father's house."

"In that, you are correct," Lady Traveston answered. "I asked Juliana to return months ago, but she's too stubborn to see reason." Her grandmother narrowed her eyes, turning back toward her. "I don't know what you were thinking. Living in a—in a fisherman's cottage."

"I live in my *father's* cottage," she pointed out. "And it never bothered me as a child." Her cheeks were burning with anger, for her grandmother had always looked down upon them. "I had a family who loved me." She hadn't needed wealth, and her mother had adored her father, despite their social differences.

Lady Traveston sighed. "And what am I? I took you in and trained you to be a lady. If it were left up to your father, you'd be nothing but a fishwife wearing rags."

Juliana took a slow breath and counted to five before she answered. "Why did you come to see me, Grandmama?"

The matron hesitated and eyed Arik, as if she suddenly realized that she'd aired out their differences in front of a stranger. She straightened and said, "My lord, I presume you know the scandal surrounding that wastrel Lord Hawthorne?"

"He abandoned his wife and son. He deserves to be—"

"Yes, yes, we know," Juliana interrupted. She didn't doubt that Arik was about to discuss slaying her husband, the enemy. "But as he has not returned, nothing can be done."

"To the contrary," Lady Traveston said. She pursed her lips as if she had tasted something that had spoiled.

"*Has* my husband returned?" Juliana demanded. Was that the reason Lady Traveston had made such a journey?

Her grandmother ignored the question. "Lord Thorgraham, perhaps you can intervene on my granddaughter's behalf to extricate her from this mess." She paused a moment and added, "If you are in need of a wife yourself, *you* might consider her."

Juliana's cheeks burned at the thought, but she said, "Grandmama, I do not think that the Duke of Somerford's son is lacking in candidates for a wife." Which was true, but she didn't at all believe that Arik was the missing heir.

Even now, he leaned against the arm of the fragile chair, and it was a wonder the wood didn't break. With his primitive clothing and the leather braces upon his muscular forearms, he appeared like an ancient barbarian.

His eyes stared into hers with interest, as if he was thinking about the stolen night they'd shared. Juliana's skin grew sensitive, and she imagined this man's hands upon her again. He had touched her without mercy, caressing her until she'd been overwhelmed by the molten desire he'd awakened.

It embarrassed her to realize that yes, she still wanted Arik. He had made her feel alive during that night, and she'd welcomed his body as he'd joined with her. William had flattered her, yes, but he'd never kindled any sort of strong desire.

You were never his wife. His mistress, perhaps, but nothing more.

Marcus's accusations haunted her still. Juliana looked away from both of them, for in the presence of Arik Thorgrim, she could not trust herself. He was the sort of man who would carry off the woman he wanted, demanding that she surrender to his seduction.

And sadly, never in her life had she enjoyed surrendering quite so much.

Stop this, she warned herself. *William could still be alive. You are hardly better than an adulteress.*

"I cannot remarry, and you know this, Grandmama." Juliana stood and paced. "At least…not until this matter is settled."

Lady Traveston sighed. "Well, we shall see about that."

Arik moved to stand behind her. The steadiness in his expression was a promise of his protection. Though he remained silent, she saw that he had no intention of abandoning her—even though she'd demanded that he do so.

Her husband had been the sort of man to walk away when responsibility called. He'd visited her at Hawthorne House when it was convenient for him, but he'd left her alone before he'd learned of her pregnancy.

Juliana suspected that Arik Thorgrim would cut down any man who dared to harm her or her son. Something within her warmed to it, especially when he touched his palm to her back.

At that moment, the butler arrived to announce dinner, and Arik escorted her inside.

"Do you know," Lady Traveston continued, "in spite of your disheveled appearance, I *like* you, Thorgraham. You appear to be a man of honor, though a trifle stoic." She took his other arm. "And a man who knows when to keep silent is one who truly listens."

Arik sent her grandmother a devastating smile, which made the older woman blush.

"Yes," Lady Traveston said to him. "I like you very much indeed."

Arik didn't recognize half the foods placed before him. There was a green stew, which was some sort of vegetable, and a round piece of bread. He picked up the chicken and bit into it, only to notice that Juliana was shaking her head at him. Lady Traveston wasn't watching either of them but had closed her eyes, savoring the first bite of food. "Ah, it is wonderful to have sustenance after a long day of traveling." She turned her back to Arik, asking her granddaughter more questions, but he hardly understood any of their conversation.

While he tore off another piece of chicken, he saw Juliana gesturing toward a strange metal object with tines. He had seen it once before at Juliana's house, but had not known what it was for.

It was then that he realized they were using knives and the strange metal tool to eat. Though he was unaccustomed to it, he supposed he could use the blade. He sliced off a bit of the chicken breast and stabbed it with the tip of his knife. While he ate, he noticed Juliana staring at him with dismay.

She lifted up the metal tool with tines, demonstrating its use. Arik didn't see a reason why it mattered, but he wiped his hands upon the cloth covering the table and reached for it.

"Juliana, are you quite well?" her grandmother was asking. "You look positively wretched."

"I—I'm fine, Grandmama. The food is very good. Nicer than I've had in months."

The matron's face darkened. "If you had come to live with me, instead of being so obstinate, you would have dined like a baroness. But I suppose you preferred *fish.*" She spoke the word as if it were a poison. Juliana brought her attention back to the plate, biting her lip as if to stop herself from speaking.

After that, Lady Traveston talked unceasingly. From the strained expression on Juliana's face, it was undoubtedly advice she didn't want to hear. Arik tried eating with the tool that he learned was a fork, and in the meantime, he listened to a conversation that he didn't really understand. Something about runners and investigations and marriage registries. Then, too, it seemed that the Anglo-Saxon tongue was easier to comprehend when he let his thoughts drift. He nodded and smiled on occasion but volunteered nothing on his own.

"Regardless of your disastrous choices, you must consider your son in all of this," the old woman informed her granddaughter. "Think of Harry's needs, not your own." Lady Traveston dabbed at her lips with a white cloth. "He's a boy who needs to be in school. I could hire tutors for him, and when he's of age, he will attend Eton."

Juliana lowered her eyes. "And what if they accuse him of being a bastard, Grandmama? How can he hold his head up among the others?"

"We will solve that dilemma when it comes to that." But the look on Lady Traveston's face held concern. She turned back to Arik. "Will you use your influence to help my granddaughter?"

He had no idea what she wanted from him, but he nodded.

"Good." The matron nodded with satisfaction before continuing, "I know that there is a great deal the pair of you haven't told me. For someone who returned from his journey so recently, I find it very intriguing that you chose to spend your first evening home with my granddaughter instead of your father." Her pointed look held a silent warning.

Arik suspected that his days with Juliana would end at

the next full moon, as her maid had predicted. These last moments were meant to be savored, lived to the fullest until they ended. There was a reason why the gods had healed his wounds, though he knew it not. He had been given a second chance at life, but he had to fight with honor, to prove himself worthy of Valhalla.

"Am I correct in assuming that you were friends before this?" Lady Traveston prompted.

"We were, yes," he answered. He studied the young woman's face, and Juliana's gray eyes suddenly locked with his, pleading with him not to say more. It was clear that the older woman's presence was weighing heavily upon her. And he sensed that Lady Traveston would become an enemy or an ally, depending on his actions.

"Lady Traveston, I should return to my father now," he lied. "I offer you my thanks for the food."

"It was my pleasure," she answered. "We will be sure to pay a call upon you and His Grace, the Duke of Somerford, in the near future. Perhaps after we've finished our business in London." Lady Traveston gave a slight wave of her hand in dismissal.

Juliana stood and said, "I will walk out with you, Lord Thorgraham."

He waited for her to join him, and she reached out to take his arm. The touch of her hand against him was light, but he could see that she was nervous around him.

She kept the pace slow, and when a footman waited near the door, she gave him a silent command to leave them alone.

"You're upset," he said in Norwegian, keeping his voice just above a whisper.

"I don't know what I am," she whispered back. "But it is becoming clearer that you are not the duke's son." She stopped in front of the staircase, resting her arm against the post.

"I told you this already, *kjære*."

She lowered her gaze, as if she was too afraid to say anything else. Arik leaned in. "I will go to the chamber you told me about. We will talk more when we are alone." He stole a kiss and took the stairs, turning the corner.

When he reached the top of the stairs, he glanced down the hall to ensure that no one was watching. Then he overheard Juliana opening and closing the front door, as if he'd gone. He counted the doorways until he reached the one Juliana had told him about. He was about to open it, when suddenly he realized that she was unlikely to come and speak with him there.

It was better to await her within the bedchamber that adjoined her room, the one that had belonged to her husband.

He remembered which room it was and found that the interior was dark, with no fire upon the hearth. Arik listened for the sound of any servants who might intrude. When there was no one, he moved toward the hearth and built a fire within it. A small blaze illuminated the space, and he opened the door that led to Juliana's room. Inside, she had a vast bed of her own with a canopy and long curtains.

He lay down and spread out his arms and legs, reveling in the softness of her mattress. This was a luxury he'd never imagined, and he preferred it to any pallet he had tried.

The hours crept on, and he closed his eyes. Likely Lady Traveston was here with the intention of taking Juliana and her son away from their home. Given the woman's jewels and her strong manner of speaking, he was certain she was a woman of wealth. But even if Juliana and Harry were safe and cared for, their land was still in the hands of an enemy. He had to find out how to get it back.

Juliana was worried about her future, but she was entirely too soft about the matter. If someone had taken this home from her, she needed to take it back with force of her own. And yet, he did not understand this world. It seemed that men fought with words instead of weapons. And even if he did successfully conquer these lands, he might not be here to ensure that Juliana kept them.

A pang of frustration tightened inside him. He liked this woman's courage and the way she had stood up to him. She had honor and loyalty. If she had belonged to him, he would enjoy awakening beside her or even giving her more children. Her blond hair would spill over her shoulders, tangling against him, if they slept together.

She should have another man to protect her—someone whose life wasn't going to disappear when the moon grew full in the sky. The thought sent a dark fury through Arik, for he didn't want another man to have that right.

The raw frustration continued to brew within his veins, minute by minute, until at last Juliana entered her room. She didn't appear to notice him until he sat up on the bed.

"Arik," she breathed. "What are you doing here?"

He crossed the room and answered her words with a kiss. Her startled mouth was open, and he claimed her, lifting her into his arms. She let out a slight cry of surprise, but he continued to kiss her.

Tonight, he intended to mark her, to brand her with the memory of him. If he had to leave when the moon turned, he wanted her to think of him with longing.

"You shouldn't be here," she whispered, as he pressed her back upon her bed. "Someone might find you."

A knock sounded at the door, and Juliana leaped up, drawing the bed curtains closed to hide him. He stared at the fabric with amusement, wondering why Juliana had not simply sent the servant away. But a moment later, the maid entered. It soon became clear that the girl had come to undress Juliana for bed. From behind the heavy curtains, he caught a clear glimpse of Juliana's nape and the complicated ties that bound her underclothing. The serving girl unlaced her, until she stood in a white garment.

He grew aroused watching, knowing that she was aware of his presence. The maid continued to undress Juliana, and Arik glimpsed her bare back before the maid lowered a creamy linen gown over her.

"Shall I turn down the bed, my lady?" the maid asked.

"No!" Juliana protested. "That is, no, thank you. I intend to sit by the fire for a while. Just leave it, if you please."

She dismissed the maid and sat upon the chair. Wearing only the white garment, she appeared vulnerable. As if she knew what could happen between them.

Arik opened the bed curtains and eyed her. "Come here," he commanded in a low voice.

She stood facing him, and the delicate fabric shadowed her lithe body. For endless minutes, she didn't move, but her gray eyes locked with his. "I have to travel to my son in the morning," she told him. "My grandmother is taking us to stay with her in London."

"I will accompany you as your guard," he said, but she shook her head.

"After tonight, you must go your way. As I must go mine." She stood and crossed the room to stand before him. "And when you've gone, I'll wonder if I only dreamed of you."

He traced the edge of her jaw, moving his hand over her throat. In the moonlight, she appeared like a goddess. Her hair was now unbound, and he stole a lock, bringing it to rest over her breasts.

"I was sent to you for a reason," he said. "You know this."

She faced him with those quiet gray eyes, and there was a softness around her. "I tell myself all the explanations, but none of them make any sense. Except the one that is impossible."

Her hands moved upon his heart, her eyes downcast. He sensed that she desired him in the same way, but there was only farewell in her posture.

He moved his hands to her waist. "It may be impossible, but can you not see what is before you?"

"I see a stranger."

"You see a man who desires you." He caressed her hips, drawing her close so that she could not deny the truth. "And you know what it feels like when I touch you."

She closed her eyes, and he spied the rise of gooseflesh upon her skin. "I'm afraid," she admitted.

"My life and yours are intertwined, though your world is not mine. I have seen mysteries that I cannot understand." His hands slid up her torso, resting alongside her breasts. He wanted to strip away this garment, to bare her skin and taste it. "I understand what a man feels with a beautiful woman, and I want to savor whatever moments I have left."

She remained quiet but didn't ask him to leave. He

wanted to lie beside her this night, to touch her. The thought of not seeing her again brought a strange sense of loss.

"I worry about my son," she whispered. "I know that my grandmother will give us a place to stay. But in London, they will label him a bastard. He'll be shunned by other boys his age."

When she pressed her cheek against his heart, he brought his arms around her. Her hair smelled faintly of flowers, and he stroked it back. "If anyone spoke ill of my son, I would confront the boys' fathers. Or I would teach my boy how to defend himself."

"You'd give him a knife," she remarked, and he detected a note of disapproval in her voice.

"Or teach him to use his fists." He drew his hand down her spine, keeping her close. "Let him fight his own battles, and he will win the respect of others."

"Harry isn't a bastard," she insisted. "I married William. And even if there is no register to prove it, I meant the vows I spoke."

He understood that this was a matter of honor to her. "And do you wish your husband was here with you now?"

She let out a rough sigh. "No. I wish I could prove that Harry is his legal heir. But I would rather be his widow than his wife." Pulling back, her gray eyes stared into his. "Is that wrong of me?"

"He is dead," Arik insisted. "Or he would have returned to you." He pulled her arms around his neck, bringing her so close, he could feel every curve of her body. "And I do not intend to let you go to London alone, Juliana."

"My grandmother won't allow you to come with us. Especially not after I said you were the duke's son." She moved her hips against his, as if trying to pull back, but the motion was even more arousing. "You will have to stay here."

"Try and stop me." He lifted her into his arms and held her tightly. She started to protest, but then he pressed her down upon the bed. "I take what I want, Juliana. I don't ask."

CHAPTER SIX

B eing at this Viking's mercy was both terrifying and provocative. She knew he wanted to lie in her arms and join with her again. The memory of this man made her ache, craving the pleasure he'd given her before.

Arik Thorgrim confused her. He was hard-headed and arrogant, but he was far more intelligent than other men she'd met. He was a man of strategy, one who knew how to read people. And God help her, he seemed to see beneath her protests.

She did want him, despite all the reasons this was wrong. He was more alive than any other man she'd met. None of the gentlemen of the ton would behave in this way. They would court a woman by dancing with her or asking permission to call upon her.

Arik Thorgrim would never ask. It was not only his primitive mannerisms or his clothing. Everything about this man spoke of a warrior. And yet, he had never once harmed her. He was strong enough to overpower her at any moment, but he had not done so. He possessed the honor William had lacked.

When his mouth descended to her throat, her body

cried out to steal a selfish moment with him. To take the pleasure he offered and give it in return.

He moved to sit beside her, before he guided her to stand up. "Take off the gown."

A shiver of anticipation rippled through her at the thought of surrendering to him. *Yes,* her body cried out, while her brain refused to yield.

You could still be married, her conscience protested. She didn't know for certain if William was dead. And despite her body's reckless needs, she did not want to be an adulteress.

"I can't," she whispered. "If I do this, it's a betrayal of my husband."

"In my land, if a wife is abandoned, she may divorce him and take another husband. The freedom is hers."

"Here, a wife is treated as her husband's property," Juliana countered. "And the choices I make will affect my son." If anyone discovered them together, it would lend credence to Marcus's insistence that she had only been William's mistress. She was not an immoral woman, nor could she surrender to desires that would bring about her ruin.

"Do you believe your husband is dead?" Arik asked.

She wanted to believe it. After so many years, the courts had declared Marcus as the guardian of the estates. Her husband's brother was now, for all practical purposes, the Viscount Hawthorne.

"I think he must be," she answered at last. "But it doesn't mean I can allow myself to be seduced." Even if William was dead, she had to be a model of propriety for Harry's sake so that no one could point an accusing finger at her. But more than that, she was afraid of unlocking her own desires and reaching for the man she truly wanted.

Arik twisted a lock of her hair, touching it as if it were

spun from silk. The look in his eyes held the promise of a sinful night, one she would never forget.

"Do you wish I had never touched you?" he asked, his voice low and deep.

His words were like a physical caress, luring her into temptation. "No." She forced herself to meet his brown eyes. "I enjoyed being with you, though it was wrong." The intensity in his gaze unnerved her. He looked as if he wanted to remove every barrier between them.

She reached out to touch his rough wool tunic. Arik guided her hand beneath it to his bare skin. She traced the scars of battle that edged his ribs.

Viking, her instincts warned.

"Are you real?" she whispered. "Sometimes I wonder if I'm going mad."

"Do I feel real to you?"

He did. The hot skin beneath her palm burned her blood in a different way. He was so unlike William. When she'd married her husband, she'd done everything possible to please him, but he had grown bored of her within a matter of months.

"I don't understand how any of this could have happened," she murmured. "I don't know who you are."

"But you know how I make you feel." His wicked hands caressed her spine, finding a sensitive place. A tremor caught within her, and for a moment she almost believed in magic. She rested her palms upon his chest and could feel his heart beating. The warm male skin tempted her to press her mouth against him.

He removed his tunic, revealing a body that had been honed like a blade. The scars he carried revealed a man who fought and bled for others.

"Let me be with you this night," he urged, running his hands down her throat to her tightening breasts.

She could say nothing, but instead, she captured his palms and held them upon her body. "I'm afraid." Afraid of the way he made her feel and the way she responded to him. This man tempted her like no other.

"I will never hurt you, Juliana." He drew his hands around her waist, keeping her close. "But I will hurt anyone who tries to take what belongs to you or your son. They will bleed for it."

His conviction was undeniable, and a sudden fear iced through her. "You cannot kill anyone."

"What I do matters not, for my life is already lost, Juliana. Soon enough, I will die. And this time, it will be over."

Somehow, he believed this. And though she could not understand how anyone could be brought across time, there was no denying that he was vastly different from any man she'd ever met. He was bold and unyielding, a man who would fight for what he wanted. He was a man of action, not words.

More than that, he made her feel alive in a way no one ever had. With him, she could speak her mind, saying whatever she wanted. He seemed to admire it, and when she'd lost her temper, his eyes had narrowed with unmistakable interest. And God help her, she wanted him, too. It simply wasn't fair that she'd married a man who had used and discarded her. And now that she'd met Arik Thorgrim, she felt as if the chains of her old life were breaking. He made her want a different life, one where *she* was in command of her choices.

Her hands curled against his chest, and she insisted, "None of us can know our fate. You—you might stay." Blood rushed to her cheeks, for she didn't know what he would think of that.

"Do you want me to stay?" His wide palms moved

down her back, pulling her to sit on his lap. There was no denying that he was a strong man, far more imposing than any of the gentlemen she knew.

In his presence, she felt vulnerable. Arik Thorgrim knew how to unsettle her, how to tempt her wilder side. Nothing about this man was tame.

I take what I want, Juliana. I don't ask.

Could he be real? Was there truth to what he was saying, that he had died in another time and could not move on yet?

Or was this the purgatory the clergymen spoke of? To die and be trapped between Heaven and earth, forced to live another life that wasn't his?

She didn't know—but selfishly, she wanted Arik to stay.

Juliana reached up and traced the scar upon his throat. "Why do you even bother with me? I am no one to you."

"You know this is not true." He caught her hand and passed it across his lips. A rush of feelings poured over her, and she wished she could rest her head against his chest and be held so tightly she could hardly breathe. No one had ever looked at her like this. Her heart was falling hard for a man she hardly knew. But there was no denying the connection she felt with him.

"My afterlife depends upon winning this battle for you," he said. But his words had nothing to do with the way he was touching her. His hands slid through her hair, and, seated on his lap, she could feel the evidence of his rock-hard desire.

He kissed her then, his mouth silencing her. Her heart quaked, and he moved his hips so she felt his arousal pressed intimately.

"Kiss me back," he ordered.

She surrendered beneath the onslaught of his mouth,

accepting the heat of his lips and tongue. Desire roared through her, and she struggled against her conscience and the way this man made her feel.

Never once had he criticized her, making her feel awkward or disappointing. He behaved as if he couldn't get enough of her. When she touched her tongue to his, he adjusted her position on his lap until she was straddling him. His hands clenched her hips, and he forced her to feel the length of his desire through the barriers of clothing. She could imagine his body thrusting within her slick entrance, and how it would feel to ride him.

She was shuddering, her breathing hitched as she sat upon him, wrapping her legs around his waist. Her nightdress was riding up against her thighs, but she hardly cared. She was drowning in need, reveling in his touch. When she tightened her legs around him, he groaned.

"Temptress," he accused, his breath heated against her mouth. "I could take you right now," he said.

She was aching for him, so wet it would take nothing at all to drive her wild. She needed to stop this madness, right now, before she did something she would later regret.

"Did you ever have a wife?" she asked, as she arched her hips against him. His eyes were smoldering, and it gave her a heightened sense of power.

He palmed her breasts, stroking the tips with his fingers. She let out a shattered breath and between her thighs, she felt the echo of his caress.

"No. The woman I loved betrayed me with another man," he told her. He continued to tease her nipples through the fabric, and she rewarded him by grinding her hips against him. A flare of jealousy caught her, at the idea of Arik loving someone else.

Which was so very foolish. Of course he'd had

another life, so long ago. But she couldn't stop the possessive desires that caught her.

"She was with another man," he said. "I tried to kill him, and his brother buried his ax in my spine."

He kept his expression neutral, as if nothing were amiss. And yet she knew that his death should not have happened that way.

"My men were taking my body back to my brother's settlement for a true burial. They all knew I would die on board the ship."

"You deserved better than a woman like that." She kissed him softly, and he returned it with tenderness of his own.

There was an unnamed emotion in his eyes when he drew his arms around her. "I thought I loved her. And yet... I don't even miss her."

She pressed her cheek against his, holding him close. It was so wrong to be with him in this way, but she could not stop herself.

"I remember looking up at the moon on the night I died, wishing I had another chance at life." He drew back, still keeping his arms around her. "The gods granted my wish. And I am grateful for the days I spent with you, Juliana of Arthur."

A sense of foreboding filled her at the thought of him leaving. It wasn't only the way he had touched her. It was the way he'd barreled into her world, demanding to fight her enemies. And the way he'd made her laugh, teaching her the joy of sailing.

And the softness in his eyes when he spoke to her son.

God help her, she could sense the heartbreak that was coming. She had to shield herself from that to protect her wayward feelings.

He drew her hands downward to rest upon his chest.

Beneath her fingers, she felt the pulse of his life. "I am not real, Juliana. I died that night. And for some reason, I am caught between life and death. The gods granted my request for a little more time, and I must honor that. If I help you and bring back your son's inheritance, it gives me a purpose. A way of redeeming the mistakes I made in my life."

Although the room was now warm, Juliana felt the chill of his words and the hint of sadness within them. He drew her hand to his chest, and his hardened muscles were warm beneath her touch. "You know that I am not a part of this life. I cannot be." He leaned in, his breath warm against her cheek. "But I intend to enjoy whatever moments I have left."

This man terrified her, not because she feared he would harm her—but because of the way he affected her feelings. He was unpredictable, barbaric...and yet he possessed more honor than any man she'd known.

"I want to touch you all night until you cry out with your need," he murmured, his mouth grazing her jaw. "The way you did before."

Between her legs, she grew wet and aching. Dear God, she did want to lie with this man again. He had made her into a wanton, desiring something she should never give. But it was more than carnal needs. She wanted to seize a memory for herself, to touch this man as he had touched her. William had been gone for so long, he might never return.

She'd been so naïve the day she'd wed him, believing that they were eloping at Gretna Green. But there was no evidence at all that she'd signed a marriage registry. It could have been a false document, for all she'd known. And at the age of eighteen, how was she to know any better?

It was tearing her up inside, and she wished that she had never married William. And yet, she couldn't regret Harry. He was the darling of her life, the son whose smile never failed to warm her. If it turned out that she and William had never been married, Harry's life would be shadowed by illegitimacy. And she didn't want him to suffer the embarrassment of his mother's mistakes.

She was falling beneath the spell of this Viking, wanting so badly to forget the years of hardship. William had never caressed her like this, nor had he cared about bringing her pleasure. He only took what he wanted.

You should be grateful that I rescued you from the life you had, her husband had told her, when he'd taken her virginity on their wedding night. *Now you will learn how to be a proper wife, one who knows her place.*

She shuddered at the memory, pushing it back.

Her fingers dug into Arik's hair when he slid her nightgown over her shoulders, revealing her bare breasts. His mouth moved downward, and she was helpless to do anything but gasp when he kissed her nipple. A violent tremor rocked through her, and he was merciless in the way he exposed her, finding all of her buried needs. "Your husband never touched you like this, did he?"

"N-no." Words of protest came back to her, but her body refused to let her speak. This man was taking apart her senses, shattering the boundaries between them.

"He turned his back on you, leaving you alone for six years. He doesn't deserve your loyalty."

Her mind and body warred with one another, and she found it difficult to breathe while he was touching her. She wanted him so badly, desiring another night in his arms. His mouth was drawing at her nipple, evoking a need that was so strong, her hands gripped his hair.

All she had to do was cast aside her morals and lie

with him. The thought was so tempting, she wanted to seize these last moments.

Because she believed that Arik *was* going to leave her. The belief struck her like a physical blow. And what would happen if she succumbed to him? He would leave, and only shattered pieces of her life would remain.

Her eyes welled up with the knowledge that once again, she would be left behind. She had relied on others for so long, letting them manipulate her life until it was no longer her own.

What kind of a woman was she? Was she truly such a shadow that she would stand back while this man left her, too? She didn't like the person she had become, a woman with no substance or backbone.

This man had drawn out a fire in her that had been lost for so long. And suddenly, she realized that he was right. William didn't deserve her loyalty. He had abandoned her for years, and no one believed he was alive. Was she meant to sacrifice the remaining years of her life, waiting for him to return? What if he never did? What if he *was* dead?

"I was sent to you, *kjære*," he said. "And I want this night with you, so you will remember me when I am gone."

Her hair had fallen around her shoulders, and Arik's eyes were heated with raw desire. Her lips were bruised and swollen, but she took a deep breath. "You were angry with your woman for betraying you with your friend. If I lie with you, am not guilty of the same sins?"

His hands froze upon her, and his expression grew hard. "It is not the same. I would not have left a wife for six years. Such would not be fair to her." He stared into her eyes. "If she took another man in my place, I would understand this. So should he."

She was beginning to wonder. William *had* walked away from her. He didn't want her as his wife, and he'd repeatedly told her how disappointed he was in her. All he had done in the six months of their marriage was train her in obedience. And she'd loathed every minute of it.

She reached out to Arik's face, touching his cheek. If she had been wedded to a man like this, she would have grieved at his loss. He had filled an empty space inside of her, giving her a strength she'd forgotten.

This time, she kissed him, and he answered it with a hunger of his own. She could barely hold a conscious thought as he held her bottom and discarded the rest of his clothing. Her nightgown fell to the floor, and they were now skin to skin. He sat down again on the bed, turning her and guiding her to lie down. She was exposed to him, and he gazed down at her body as if he intended to conquer her.

"So beautiful," he said, as he reached to touch her breasts. "I would never have left a woman like you behind." He grazed the tips of her hardened nipples with his thumbs, circling them as he drew her hips to the edge of the bed. She was dizzy with the sensations, and she gasped when he slid the tip of his manhood inside her. Though she tried to bring him deeper, he withheld himself. The sensation only made her anticipate his thrusts, but he only remained there, waiting.

"He hurt you like this, didn't he?" Arik murmured. "You took no pleasure in your marriage bed."

"It stopped hurting after a while," she admitted. "He wasn't happy with me and said I needed to be taught."

The expression on his face darkened, and he withdrew from her body. Juliana wasn't certain what she'd done wrong, but he lay down beside her, drawing her to face him. "In my country, if a man does not satisfy his woman, she will take another man as her husband."

He took her hand in his and demanded, "Tell me where you want to be touched."

Her face flooded with color. "I don't know. I don't know any of this or what I should do. That night on the ship—you did everything." She had surrendered completely, letting him take command. And the raw sensations had taken her into a storm of physical bliss.

Arik took her hands and placed them upon his chest. "And what if I let you do whatever you wish to me? Would you prefer to have all the power, *kjære*?"

The idea had never occurred to her. Without waiting for her answer, he lifted her easily, letting her straddle his body. Then he leaned back with both hands behind his head.

She was tentative at first, touching his hair and then his face. Never had she expected him to let her take the lead. But it seemed that Arik was a man who wanted her to enjoy sharing his bed.

Her palms moved over his broad shoulders, tracing the scars that covered his skin. His stomach was flat and hard, and she hesitated at his waist.

"Go on," he urged.

She touched his erection, startled at the heat and hardness of him. His skin was smooth, and when she touched the head of him, a bead of moisture was there. Curious, she rubbed it, and his fingers dug into the coverlet, his body tensing.

"By the gods," he gritted out.

"Did I hurt you?" She pulled back her hands, but he shook his head.

"Again, *kjære*. Do whatever you wish, as long as you wish."

She held him in her fist, moving her hand up, caressing him with her thumb before she moved it down again. His face tensed, but she realized that she was giving him pleasure. He was moving in counterpoint to her, and as she moved her hand up and down, he grew slick in her palm.

The motion began to arouse her, as she imagined what it would be like to feel his length embedded within her. She remembered how delicious it had felt when he had slid only a fraction inside her.

What if she did the same to him? She eased up on her knees, still stroking him with her hand, and then she poised above him. His dark eyes flew open, and he nearly let out a growl when she took him barely inside her.

She was so wet, so eager to move against him, it took control to give in to the temptation. But instead of being angry with her, he gave a wicked smile. "You think to torment me, do you?" With that, he balanced his weight on his hands and sat up so he could take her nipple in his mouth. He sucked hard, and she clenched his shaft in response.

Oh dear God, she needed this. She needed him to move within her, to take her past the brink. But all he did was continue to lick and suckle at her nipples.

He tongued the other breast, and she sank down upon him, embedding him fully inside her. His body stretched hers, until she could feel every inch of his hardness.

And still, he didn't move.

Slowly, she rose up and sank down upon him. It was like a physical caress, deep within.

"That's it," he encouraged. "Where do you want me to touch you now?"

She began moving in her own rhythm, slow and deep. She knew that he had more knowledge in this, and she pressed him back to the bed, still riding him. "Touch me wherever it will make me feel the most pleasure."

There was a hint of wickedness in his eyes, but he lowered his hands to the place where their bodies were joined. While he was inside her, he began stroking the hooded flesh above her entrance. Waves of sweet aching flooded through her, and she couldn't stop herself from rising up. He kept one thumb against her center, circling it, while he used his other hand to touch her breast. It was as if the two places were joined together, building higher as she arched back. She shuddered against his hand, knowing that her release was so close now.

Her heartbeat quickened, and she could feel his thickness at her entrance while she clenched him hard. He moved his hand higher, and began to rub her with the lightest pressure, faster now, until she was unable to speak or breathe. She was coming apart from the inside, a pulsing eruption claiming her.

The shimmering release caught her, unfolding like a blossom as she milked his shaft, letting him feel how much her body needed him. Never in her life had she known that making love with a man could feel this intimate.

He thrust against her, and took his own pleasure, grinding against her until he spilled his seed. She lay down against him, his body still within hers.

Her eyes welled up, and she knew her foolish heart was falling fast. She had become intimate with a man who never cared if she argued with him or dared to touch him. With him, she could be a strong woman who did as she pleased. If she stayed near him for very long, she would be vulnerable to her feelings. And she feared he was right, that he could not possibly remain with her.

She closed her eyes, wondering what she'd done.

She'd mistakenly believed that she could take this night with him to prove to herself that she was no longer bound by William. That she would let go of her past and move forward with her life, making her own decisions.

Instead, she knew that the wiser course of action was to leave Arik Thorgrim. She withdrew from him and he rolled to the side, pulling her against him. A few hours from now, she would return to London with her grandmother.

It was the only way to protect herself from a broken heart.

*H*e was drowning. The water pulled him under so violently, he could taste the salt. His arms thrashed, and beneath the dark waves, he sensed the silent call of death.

I will not die.

He fought for every breath, and within his consciousness came the awareness that he was not alone. He struggled to move his body through the sea, while above him, the blood-red moon cast its rays upon the water.

There. A broken piece of his ship floated upon the water, and he swam as hard as he could to reach it. His fingers seized the wood, and he crawled upon it, his heart pounding.

All grew still, and ahead, he glimpsed the flare of a torch. The crushing weight of fear lifted, for it meant land was surely near. He closed his eyes with thankfulness, so grateful for the gift of life.

His clothing was drenched, and when his feet finally touched the ground, he lifted his face to the sky and prayed his thanks. He sank to his knees, digging his hands into the wet sand. He didn't know where he was right now...likely Norway, as he'd spent the past year sailing along the coast of Prussia, Denmark, and Finland. He wanted to go home, to see his father again and apologize for all that he'd done. He'd never have left home, were it not for his frustration at his lack of freedom.

None of that mattered now. He was alive, and though he'd never wanted to be a duke, he would accept the responsibilities he'd fled. He'd been so angry at the legacy of his forebears closing in around him...at his requirement to sit in the House of Lords, debate laws, and, of course, marry an heiress from a good family.

Now, he didn't care.

He would bind himself to the life he didn't want, if it meant he could see his father sitting by the fire, reading his favorite book, Gulliver's Travels. *He could envision the older man seated in his wingback chair, a cup of cold tea on the table beside him.*

The wind whipped at his skin, and he shivered. A dark vision came over him, of being struck in the back with an ax. A phantom pain ached, and strange words mingled within his mind. Tangled words in a language he'd not heard before...but somehow he could understand them.

Svala betrayed me.

Who was Svala? He blinked a moment, forcing himself to get up, trudging forward through the sand.

The crude houses that lay before him were not made of bricks with glass windows. These were far older, more primitive. Where was he? It was as if his life had been unseated, torn apart at the seams.

He was Eric Fielding, the Marquess of Thorgraham. And yet...he was not. Another name came into his consciousness, Arik Thorgrim. Flashes of memories intruded, memories that weren't his.

Eric tried to force them back, wondering if the violent storm had caused him to see and hear things that weren't there. God help him.

A woman emerged from the shadows. She wore a woolen gown with a long apron pinned at her shoulders by two golden brooches. She stared at him in shock, her mouth hanging open. Her golden hair hung unbound below her waist, and she whispered, "Arik... I thought you were dead."

Arik awakened in the soft bed, the dream slipping away like grains of sand. He stared at the ceiling, understanding that he had glimpsed the dream through another man's eyes.

We were switched, he realized. For some unknown reason, he had been given this life, a thousand years in the future, while the duke's son was sent back in time.

He remembered the woman who had stood upon the sand. Her name was Katarina, and she had been a friend for years. In truth, she had cast lovesick eyes upon him, though he had not returned the feelings. He'd been too blinded by Svala's fiery beauty, never recognizing her treachery.

It took long moments for the remnants of the dream to fade. His body was cold, and he could almost feel the frigid salt water clinging to his skin.

He rolled over, tangled up in the sheets. He had slept later than he'd thought, and Juliana had already risen and departed. He wished she were here, so he could curl up with her warm body. The moment he thought of touching her last night, his body grew aroused. He had wanted to awaken beside her, with her soft curves pressed against him.

He dressed quietly, realizing that the nightmare had made him lose all sense of time, for the sun was high in the morning sky. When he looked around the room, he realized that all of Juliana's belongings were gone.

His first instinct was to seek her out and bring her back...only to realize that she had likely returned to fetch Harry. After that, they would continue to London as they had planned. He knew not how he would make his way there, but he suspected the place called London was actually Lundenwic, a town his brother Magnus had raided on many occasions before he'd gained control of East Anglia.

A bitter pang caught him at the thought of his brother. They had been the best of friends, and he missed Magnus with a fierce ache. If the gods were willing, he hoped to see his brother in the afterlife that awaited him. Perhaps even his father.

He stared outside at the land and the large standing stone that had been marked with runes. So much had changed in a thousand years. The large river that had cut a path through the land had now dwindled to a small stream.

Yet the earth and sky were the same. Human needs were also the same—the desire for companionship and family. Juliana's love for her son reminded him of his own mother's love, constant and unfailing.

He wanted to help her regain all that was lost, not only for the boy's sake, but for hers. She was beautiful, strong, and loyal. A woman worth fighting for.

Although she claimed she did not need Arik's assistance, he didn't believe that. Her enemies would not give up the land without a battle. Juliana kept insisting he couldn't kill anyone, as if she expected him to hack his way through her enemies. The idea was tempting, for a dead man could not seize land. But, for her sake, he would not strike unless her enemy gave the first blow. He also needed to learn more about this man Marcus, to determine why he had stolen from Juliana's son.

He could not attack without men to help him. Lundenwic was an unknown place, and if that was where her enemy dwelled, then there he would go. His gaze rested upon the Duke of Somerford's lands. The elderly man strongly resembled his father, and possibly the man could be an ally. The vivid dream made him wonder if their parallel lives were meant to converge.

Arik slipped outside his room and down the stairs without being noticed. Years of raiding had taught him how to be nearly invisible, and he managed to leave the house like a shadow. Only when he was free of Hawthorne House did he walk openly toward the stable. The moment he stepped inside, a young lad stared at him in shock. "My—my lord, I—do you need something?"

"A horse," he answered.

The boy looked as though he were about to argue, but Arik stepped forward, using his full height to look down on him.

"Yes, my lord. Of course, you may borrow…that is, Lord Hawthorne wouldn't mind a'tall." The boy scurried to put a saddle and bridle on the gelding, while Arik waited. His presence seemed to make the lad nervous, for the boy was jabbering something about the Duke of Somerford and bringing back the horse.

"Where did Lady Traveston and her granddaughter go?" he demanded.

"Lady—that is, Miss Nelson—went to fetch her son.

And then they were going straight to London afterward, so I heard."

Which was what he'd anticipated. With a nod to the boy, Arik mounted the horse and began riding toward the stone monolith on the duke's property. Though he supposed Lady Traveston had her own servants to guard them, he didn't like leaving Juliana alone. She was a beautiful woman who would attract the eye of any man.

Arik slowed the pace of the horse after they crossed the field, and the more he thought of her, the more he tensed. She had left without a farewell, as if she did not intend to see him again. As if she wanted none of his help.

But he was not about to let her walk away. Juliana of Arthur had come to mean more to him than he'd anticipated. And if that meant seeking help from the Duke of Somerford, this he would do.

He continued on his path, imagining how his brother must have walked these lands, a thousand years ago. Though he had only visited Magnus once, this place held pieces of his brother's spirit. The loneliness caught him like a fist in his stomach, knowing that he would never again see his family alive. He forced back any emotions, unable to dwell on it. The gods had sent him through time, and once his task was completed, he would join his brother and father in the afterworld.

The duke's fortress stood on the rise of a hill. It was made of stone and was poorly guarded from what he could tell. There were no warriors, no armed men. Only a circular gravel pathway that curved before the limestone stairs.

A servant appeared, and from the moment he glimpsed Arik, his mouth dropped open. He spoke words in the Anglo-Saxon tongue that took a moment to understand.

Something about the duke's lost son being alive when they believed he was dead. He forced himself to concentrate, and slowly the meaning of the words broke forth.

"My lord, His Grace will be so glad to see you. Here, let me take your horse." The man reached for the horse's reins. "Go on inside, and Mr. Nolan will see to you."

Arik remained wary, but he dismounted and approached the stairs while the man saw to his horse. Before he reached the doorway, it opened, and another servant greeted him. Once again, it seemed that they believed he was the duke's son, and he did not deny it. He wanted to speak with Somerford, and if omitting the truth would help him, so be it.

They were about to lead him toward another room, but he saw the older man standing at the far end of the hall. The moment the duke laid eyes upon Arik, his eyes turned troubled. Although Arik's appearance had deceived the servants, both of them were aware that he wasn't the man's son.

"So, you've returned," the duke said. "I was hoping you would."

"We should talk," Arik said. "Without the others around us."

The duke nodded for Arik to follow him, and once they were inside a smaller room, he closed the doors. The walls were made of wood panels, and there were leather-wrapped manuscripts lining the space.

For a moment, Arik was reminded of the dream he'd had. Across the room, he spied a wingback chair with a table beside it—the same furnishings he'd seen in his dream. A chill rose over him with the realization that the visions he'd had were another man's memories. More and more, he was growing convinced that he had somehow switched places in time with the duke's son.

For a time, the duke stared at him. It was as if he couldn't quite believe what he was seeing. Arik struggled to remember the man's name. Gregory Fielding, that was it.

Gregory went to a small table and opened a door, revealing the sack that contained the hoard of gold and silver. He spread it out on a low table, piece by piece. Arik sat across from the man, and traced the edge of a woman's silver armband. It might have been worn by his brother's wife.

"These pieces of silver were forged hundreds of years ago," the duke guessed.

"A thousand," Arik corrected. "They belonged to my—" He was about to say brother, but realized how it would sound to the man. "—to someone I knew once," he amended.

"I do not know how you knew they were buried on my land or why you gave me half. You could have taken all of the treasure for yourself and not told me of it. I want to know why." The duke's voice was cool, and yet, there was unrest within his tone.

"Because you were meant to have it," Arik answered. There was no other reason he could give. How could he tell this man that he'd felt an instinctive need to give away half his brother's hoard? But he added, "You remind me of my own father."

"My servants believe you are my son, returned to me. You do look like him." There was a trace of worry in his voice, as if he didn't trust his eyes. Surely the man understood that Arik was not his son, didn't he? Beyond the questions, he saw the desperate need for hope in the older man's expression as Gregory picked up a golden brooch. "I know that you are not a bastard son, for I remained true to my wife. There is no explanation for your resemblance to Eric, except the one I wish to believe."

Arik lowered his head and said, "I am not your son." Yet, deep within him, he felt the need to offer this man something. Whatever the reason, there *was* a connection with someone else. He had dreamed visions of a different life that included this man. Somehow he possessed memories that likely belonged to the duke's son.

"Ever since I returned to these shores," Arik continued, "I have had visions that were not mine. I dreamed of this room, last night. I saw you sitting in that chair, with one of those leather manuscripts beside you. *Gulliver's Travels,* it said. And there was a cup of tea gone cold." He struggled to recall the rest of the dream. "You do not read it, do you? Your wife wrote notes to you inside the pages."

The duke said nothing, but his face blanched. "How could you know that?" For a moment, a flare of hope welled up in his brown eyes. By the gods, the man *wanted* to believe that somehow his son had returned. "No one knew that, save my son."

"As I told you, it was a dream given to me by the gods. Nothing more."

The old man stared at him for a long moment, as if searching for the truth. "I don't believe you." He opened a desk drawer, searching for something. "You must be Eric. Perhaps you were wounded and have forgotten a great deal. I have heard of circumstances like these before."

"I am not him. Some of his memories were given to me, but we are not the same."

"At first I believed that, for you dress and act like a

different man. But perhaps I was wrong." The desperate need in his eyes, to find his son, was so strong, it seemed to push away the duke's grasp upon reality.

"No," Arik said again. He didn't want Gregory to make false assumptions, when there was no chance that he was the man's son.

But the old man persisted. "Even your name, don't you see? You call yourself Arik Thorgrim, when your name is Eric Fielding, Lord *Thorgraham*. They are one and the same. Somehow you must have forgotten who you are," he insisted.

"I have not forgotten. And though you may long for his safe return, it will not happen." This man's son was lost in time, a thousand years earlier. And there was no reason to think he could come back.

The duke remained unconvinced. "But don't you see, he—"

Arik seized the man's hands and held them upon the desk. The old duke needed to face the truth, despite how harsh it was. "We were switched." He would not relinquish his grip, allowing no argument. "The gods took our spirits and switched them in time. I don't belong here, any more than he belongs in my world, with *my* family. I have his memories, and he has mine. I know this makes me sound like a man of lies, but I swear on Odin's name, that I tell you the truth. Your Eric is gone, and I am in his place."

With that, he released the duke's hands, and the old man staggered back to stand behind the desk. His eyes had widened, and he gripped the back of a chair like a shield.

"It can't be. Such things don't happen."

"No. They do not." It had taken time for Arik to accept it, but he saw no other explanation for the strange visions he had or why Gregory so strongly resembled his father. This world seemed parallel to his own, for an unknown reason.

Gregory stilled, but his eyes held weariness. "Tell me more of what you saw in your dreams."

Was it right to tell him of the strange visions? It might only heighten the man's hopes, when Arik believed the duke's son was trapped within his time.

"I do not know where the gods took your son," Arik said quietly. "But I have heard his thoughts. I sensed his spirit with me, in his words and in his voice." He took a step closer to the older man. "He was in a shipwreck, in the same storm that brought me here." He told the duke about the dream he'd had, of his son landing upon the shores of Rogaland.

"Eric always wanted to travel," the duke admitted. "He was angry with me when I wanted him to stay and accept his duties." He took an unsteady breath. "Will he return?"

Arik shook his head. "I do not believe he can." If their lives were switched at the moment of death, if they were truly caught in a world between this life and the afterlife, then there was no hope at all.

An ache caught him at the understanding that he would never be a part of Juliana's life. Once he had completed his task, he would reach the afterworld. And she would be left alone with her son.

His protective instincts sharpened. She had traveled with her grandmother, but there was no one, save the old woman's servants, to guard them. He had to find out where she had gone, and he needed the duke to help him in this.

Gregory stared at the wall for a long time, as if gathering command of his emotions. "I wanted to believe you were Eric." He closed his eyes and ran his hands through his graying hair. "I have grieved for the loss of my son, over this past year. I neglected my estates and my debts have piled up. Until you brought me this." He held up a golden brooch, and a look of regret passed over him. "I would give up every last piece of it, if I could have my son returned to me."

Seeing this man, who so strongly resembled his father, brought another ache inside Arik. He would never see his family again or feel that sense of unity among them. He'd never expected his death to bring out such regrets, but now, he wished he'd taken the time to know his father better.

"He regretted leaving in the way he did," he told Gregory. "Your son did not want to be a duke, and that is why he fled this place."

The duke did not respond at first. He was tracing his hands over the gold, his sorrow palpable. "I suppose I always knew that. What I do not know is who *you* are. You look so much like Eric. I wish—"

"As I told you before, I am Arik Thorgrim. Valdr is my father, and I was born in Rogaland." He held the man's gaze, wondering how much the duke would believe. "I was struck down by an enemy and left to die," he admitted to the duke. "But I was given a second chance to live. I was brought by the gods to Juliana of Arthur, and I intend to help her and her son." He regarded the old man and added, "You are going to help me. That is my price for giving you half of this hoard."

Gregory frowned. "It is not my place to interfere in their lives, though William Arthur, regrettably, was not a good man. He treated her badly, and it would be better if he never came back to her. I've heard rumors that he may have returned from his travels on the Continent, but I do not know for certain."

"I hope he *does* return," Arik countered. "And if he dares to threaten her or her son, he will learn who Juliana's new protector is."

The duke studied him with interest. "You wish to take care of her, then."

Gregory made it sound as if Arik's interest lay only in Juliana. And although Arik could not deny the desire she'd kindled, it was far more than that.

"Her son deserves a better life." He closed the distance between them, feeling the anger rise up within him. "Harry is an innocent, and others took what rightfully belonged to him. We will not stand aside and let her enemies steal his lands."

A flash of unrest crossed the man's face. "I am too old to fight battles like these. But I could put in a word with my solicitor. Perhaps there is something we can do."

"She is a woman of honor and goodness," Arik insisted. "William of Arthur betrayed her, and she does not deserve that shame."

He thought of the way Juliana had held Harry's hand, walking along the shore. She had been a patient, loving mother. A woman such as Juliana deserved a man who would protect her, who could provide for both of them and defend her honor.

You cannot be that man, his conscience warned. He knew that...and yet, he held regrets. If he had his life ahead of him, he would pursue Juliana. He would give her gifts, spend hours walking with her, and try to coax a smile.

The duke sobered and nodded. "We could try."

Arik sat down across from the older man. "How will we help her? Her grandmother took her to Lundenwic. Or London, I believe you call it."

"I have a house in London," the duke said, "though I

only dwell there when I must." He let out a sigh. "Parliament will be in session soon, and I do have to go back."

"I will escort you there," Arik said. "And you will help me face Juliana's enemies."

The duke paused. "You are referring to Marcus Arthur, the acting Viscount Hawthorne." He rubbed at his chin. "Marcus is not the enemy you think he is. He allowed Juliana to stay on at Hawthorne House for many years, though he claims she was only William's mistress."

"She was the man's wife," Arik corrected.

The older man shrugged. "Wife or mistress, she cannot remain at Hawthorne House. Marcus intends to marry soon, and he cannot have Lady Hawthorne and her son in residence with his bride. But as I told you before, if the viscount *has* returned, then all can be put to rights."

"Juliana does not deserve to lose her home and lands. Someone must fight for her," Arik insisted. "And this I will do. She needs a place of her own."

The duke inclined his head, but his face held that same sense of regret. "You do remind me of my son. He never stood by and allowed injustice to happen." He stood and added, "I suppose I could let you come to London with me. Since you gave me this treasure, it's a reasonable request." He beckoned in a silent command for Arik to follow. "But we should find some better clothes for you, if you intend to confront Lord Hawthorne."

Arik eyed the duke's attire, wondering why any man would bother with a knotted cloth around his neck. But he did understand that he had to blend in with the other men, in order to better understand Juliana's enemy. "As you say."

They left the room, and Arik followed the duke up a

staircase. When they reached the landing, the older man turned back. There was a wistful expression in his eyes, and he admitted, "I still want to believe that you are my son. Others will believe it, and you must be prepared for that. If you truly want to help Lady Hawthorne, you must pretend to be Eric."

"Such is not necessary." Arik had no intention of stealing another man's name or place. "They will understand that it is a resemblance, nothing more." He didn't want the duke believing that he was here to usurp the young man's place.

But Gregory was already shaking his head in denial. "If you want my help in regard to Lady Hawthorne, you will have no choice but to deceive everyone. You may borrow some of my son's clothing, and I will let them believe that you are Eric, returned from your journey." He thought a moment and nodded. "I think enough of my friends will accept it, and it will allow you to see Lady Hawthorne."

"Tell me more about her husband," Arik commanded. He felt that Juliana had not revealed everything to him.

The duke crossed his arms and admitted, "The viscount was a reckless sort, dallying with anyone in skirts. Lady Hawthorne deserved better than him. He left for the Continent nearly six years ago, I think. I don't know if he stayed away by choice or whether he was prevented from returning because of the war."

"*Is* he her husband? Does he have the right to claim her?"

The duke sent him a curious look. "I do not know. But Lady Hawthorne does not appear to be a silly girl who would have succumbed to a seduction. She believed it was a true marriage and behaved like a model wife, whether or not Hawthorne deceived her."

The thought didn't sit well with Arik, for he didn't want to believe that Juliana had ever belonged to another man. If Hawthorne did come back to her, she would have no choice but to return to her husband. The thought burned him like a searing flame, for he wanted no other man to touch Juliana in the way he had.

"Why does she not end the marriage and divorce him?" Arik asked.

"She stays for the sake of her son," the older man answered. "She cannot divorce William, or she would lose everything."

He loathed the idea of Juliana returning to a marriage with a man who had mistreated her. In many ways, life was far easier a thousand years ago. She could have ended the marriage and taken another man as her husband. A man like him.

Arik wouldn't have minded coming home to her each night, sharing her bed and taking care of Juliana. He would have enjoyed teaching her son how to hunt and fish. Any man would be proud of such a boy, and he could understand Juliana's need to protect him.

You will not be here to guard him, his conscience chided. *You are already dead.*

The thought was sobering. All his life, he'd wasted years fighting enemies, raiding along the coastlines of foreign lands.

But now, he had people to fight for. Not only to secure his place in the afterworld, but because he wanted to give Juliana and her son a better life before he left them.

Perhaps that was what had been missing from his life—a reason to fight. But even if he did win this battle for them, he found that he was reluctant to leave them behind. The days he'd spent with Juliana had had a comforting familiarity, and the boy had given him a taste of what it would be like to be a father.

He knew, deep inside, that he could not share a life with Juliana. Time was slipping away from him, and soon enough, his soul would disappear. Thinking of her was not wise, for it could only end in bitter separation.

"If it is Juliana's wish to end the marriage to Hawthorne, then I will help her to do so," he said. Whether that meant challenging the man in battle or by another means, he intended for her to hold the power.

"She does not have that right," the duke answered. "At least, not yet." A spark seemed to light up the man's eyes, as if he were embarking upon an adventure. "You did aid me in a time of need. If your only desired compensation is to help Lady Hawthorne, then I see no reason why I should not lend you my assistance—though you have much to learn about London society." His gaze focused upon Arik, and he nodded. "A great deal, indeed. I suspect a man like you has never set foot inside a ballroom. But I believe we can help Lady Hawthorne."

Arik reached out to grasp the man's hand. "Teach me what I need to know."

ChAPTER SEVEN

TWO WEEKS LATER

Juliana could hardly keep her eyes open. After all the days of traveling with Harry, Grelod, and her grandmother, she was ready to lay her head upon the dining room table and sleep for hours. She picked at her food, and inwardly, she felt a sense of disquiet. She'd grown so accustomed to Arik Thorgrim, her life felt empty without him. Even Harry had complained that he missed the man.

Sometimes she stumbled between fantasy and reality. In her head, she knew that it was impossible for any man to travel through time. But her heart said otherwise. She had shared two nights with him that had broken apart the shielded edges of her feelings. For the first time in her life, she had taken a night of pleasure for herself, damning the consequences.

Juliana missed him already. She wished she had not left him behind, even knowing that Arik would slay any man alive who dared to threaten her.

Grelod was watching her intently, and there was a

dark worry on her maid's face when Juliana returned to her room. She raised her arms so the older woman could help her undress, and at last, she asked her maid what was wrong. "You've hardly spoken to me," she said. "Is it about Mr. Thorgrim?"

The older woman nodded. "I fear for your life, my lady."

Juliana smiled. "My life? For what reason? I'm perfectly well."

Her maid paled. "Forgive me, my lady, but I must ask…is it possible that you could be with child again?"

"That's impossible," Juliana protested. But the moment she voiced the words, a frigid fear passed over her. She had given herself to Arik on the night they had met and then a second time only two weeks ago.

She closed her eyes, unwilling to even think of such a thing. If the worst had come to pass—if her moment of indiscretion had resulted in a child, it would cast its shadow over Harry. Juliana gripped the edges of her nightdress, willing it not to be so. To be pregnant with another man's child, while she was trying to unravel the mystery of her marriage…it was unthinkable. She shoved back the unwelcome fear, shaking her head. "No, there is nothing of that sort."

Her menses were only a few days late, and it often happened. Surely there was no reason to worry. Though she kept her tone even, inside, the tendrils of fear took root.

"My lady, I know you do not wish to believe it, but this Viking is not of our world. On the night he came to us, I had prayed to the gods to send you a protector, someone to avenge you for what Lord Hawthorne did." Her maid looked down at her hands, her shoulders lowered. "I have had visions in the past few days, and I have foreseen that he *will* be gone when the moon turns. But if there is a child, it will bind him unnaturally to this life." Her maid gripped her hands together and said, "A dead man cannot sire a living child. It is impossible."

Juliana knew her maid believed in her visions and was more superstitious than most people. Normally, she paid little heed to Grelod's words. But this time, it was different. She now believed that Arik had traveled through time, something that she'd never imagined was possible. Her maid was right in her assertion that conceiving a child with Arik Thorgrim was unnatural.

"I don't know what to believe," Juliana admitted. But her legs were unsteady, and she took a chair, feeling faint.

"I've seen the way he looks at you," Grelod said. Her maid came forward and studied her closely. "Do not fall in love with him. He cannot stay here."

Juliana shook her head. "I am not in love with him." She had separated herself from him in an effort to hold her distance and protect her heart. But she understood Grelod's warning. Arik Thorgrim knew how to tempt her, how to bring her body such pleasure, she wanted to abandon all else for him.

She rested her hands upon her stomach, swallowing hard. *It will be all right,* she told herself. Her grandmother had agreed to give Harry and her a place, somewhere safer than her father's house. Mr. Thorgrim might have claimed that he wanted to fight her battles for her, but she didn't need him to interfere. She had left him behind, and that was that. He would go his own way, and she would go hers.

The thought shouldn't have brought such a wave of loneliness, but she could do nothing to stop it.

"If you find that you are with child, you must tell me of it immediately, my lady."

Her maid's warning held a grim note that chilled her blood. "What are you so afraid of, Grelod?"

"I'm afraid for your life," her maid admitted. "If he planted a child within you, the child might not live…and you would be in danger, my lady."

A dark fear curled up within her. Surely it could not have happened. But she could not deny the slight chance.

"We will not think of it," she insisted. "All that matters now is finding the marriage registry and proving that Harry is legitimate."

Grelod said nothing, but helped pull back the coverlet. "Your grandmother does not believe you were ever married. She brought you here to find a new husband."

Juliana didn't want to even imagine such a thing. What man would consider her for a wife now, after all the scandal she'd suffered? Moreover, she didn't trust her instincts when it came to men. She had met William on the night of her debut, and he'd flirted outrageously with her. Within a matter of days, he'd planned their elopement, and she'd agreed to it.

She had been far too naïve and innocent. Was that what had happened with Arik Thorgrim? Had she allowed her heart to lead her astray once again? Though she tried to shield her feelings, she could not stop thinking of this man. She missed his arrogance and the way he'd stared at her as if he wanted to spend every night at her side.

Her grandmother intended for her to attend several soirees and assemblies, but Juliana couldn't imagine it. She saw no reason to be dragged back into society, where people would stare at her and speak in whispers. No, she preferred to remain hidden, so no one could point fingers at her and cast blame.

You're a coward, an inner voice chided. *If you hide, they'll believe you have a reason.* If she attended as the viscountess, she could stand tall as one who had a right to be there. But if Marcus showed up and intervened... Her cheeks burned with the thought of how humiliating that would be.

A soft knock sounded on the door, and when Juliana called out for the person to enter, her grandmother walked into the bedroom.

"We must talk about tomorrow evening," she said. "I've arranged for you to attend Lady Spencer's ball. There are many older gentlemen who will attend, and one of them could be a potential husband for you. He might be willing to overlook what happened, and he could help you provide for Harry."

"I don't want to remarry, Grandmama," she reminded the matron. "And I cannot wed anyone until I know what happened with William." The idea of taking on a new household, seeing to a new husband's needs, and enduring his touch was too much to consider.

You enjoyed Arik's touch, her wicked mind insisted. *If he were your husband, you wouldn't protest at all.*

But strangely, whenever she *had* protested his actions, he'd respected her when she had stood up to him. Arik had brought out her spirit, whereas a new husband would likely suppress it.

"Everyone believes that you were William's mistress," Lady Traveston continued. "You must be prepared for that."

"I was his *wife!*" Juliana insisted. "I spoke the vows. I know what happened because I was there."

Her grandmother's face hardened. "You were a girl of eighteen. And my investigators believe that you never reached Scotland, as he told you. The church you described wasn't in Scotland—it was much farther south. And whatever vows you spoke meant nothing, because you did not have your father's permission. Your so-called marriage was invalid from the start."

"That cannot be true." Her head was beginning to ache from all of the revelations. After Marcus had thrown her out, Papa had welcomed her home and had never once spoken about the marriage. "My father never protested at all. He seemed happy when I told him about our marriage."

"Because, for a time, you had a fine home and the viscount's protection. Then, after your so-called husband went missing, you still had your freedom to live your life as you chose. At least, until a little while ago," she amended. "Why would an impoverished fisherman destroy your illusions, when you had a better life than he could give you?"

There was nothing she could say to that. Her father had never spoken of William, not when he was alive or dead. He'd refused when Juliana had invited him to come and live at Hawthorne House, claiming that he preferred to live in simplicity by the sea. Now she wondered if he'd wanted to distance himself from her husband.

If William had ever been that.

Her father's life as a fisherman had always been humble. He'd treated her mother like an angel, and they had never seemed unhappy in the years they'd had together. It was only after her mother died that Papa had sent her to visit Lady Traveston for a lady's education and for her first Season. Then, she'd learned the truth about Mama's upbringing.

"After I married William, you never wrote to me, nor did you ever visit," Juliana said to her grandmother. "I thought marrying a viscount would please you."

"You chose a charlatan and a rake," Lady Traveston answered. "I knew he would ruin you, and so he did."

She spoke as if Juliana had chosen the wrong fork instead of the wrong man. "In any account, you are quite lucky that Lady Spencer is willing to overlook your indiscretion. We will find you a husband—and this time, really, you should allow me to choose him. After that, all will be put to rights."

Juliana could hardly keep from gaping. Her grandmother expected her to stand back and let her choose a second husband, as if he were a horse?

At her silence, Lady Traveston prompted, "Well? Have you nothing to say? I do believe thanks are in order, seeing as how I'm rescuing you from that hovel."

After you left me there for the past six months, Juliana wanted to remind her. Instead, she admitted, "I don't know what to say."

"*I* think it's time that you faced the truth," Lady Traveston said. "Admit that you made a mistake and learn from it. Choose another man."

When she only shook her head, her grandmother tried again. "Your life is not over," she said gently. "You may be ruined, but there *are* men out there who will give you a second chance. A foreigner, perhaps. I suppose you won't wed anyone higher than a baronet or a knight, but there are quite a few who would be glad of a lovely wife. You aren't that bad-looking, you know."

Juliana started to shake her head, but Lady Traveston raised a hand. "Enough of this. It has been six months since you left Hawthorne House. You must let go of the past and move forward. We were fortunate that I could even get you this invitation."

Something in her grandmother's tone was strange, and Juliana suddenly questioned why Lady Traveston had waited all this time to come for her. *Something* had prompted her to travel to Norfolk, after so many years of ignoring her. A fearful premonition gripped her. "Grandmama, what has happened? Why did you really bring me here?"

"To find a husband, of course. Now, truly, you should—"

"*Why*, Grandmama? Why now?"

The matron studied her, and her overbearing demeanor suddenly softened. "Because I don't want that blackguard to get away with ruining you. You deserve a better life than the one you had."

Her stomach began to turn itself inside out as she grasped what Lady Traveston was saying. "He what? Do you mean to say that William has returned?"

Her grandmother stiffened but nodded. "He has. And apparently he is seeking a wife. I rather thought he should be held accountable for what he did." She let out a quiet sigh. "And I knew you would not believe me unless you saw him with your own eyes." Her grandmother reached out for her hand, but it brought her no comfort at all. "You will want to speak with him about what he did to you."

A dark anger rose up in the pit of her stomach. Speak with him about what he did? She wanted to drive her fist into his jaw.

Seeking a wife.

How could he have done this? And worse, how could she have been so stupid as to believe him when they'd eloped? She had wasted years of her life waiting for him to return. She had remained steadfast over the years, taking care of their son, believing that one day, all would be well. And now she realized that her indiscretion with Arik Thorgrim was nothing compared to what William Arthur had done. Doubtless he'd taken other mistresses since he'd left her. Never had he taken their marriage seriously—for it had never been a marriage at all.

All traces of her guilt were absolved now. She had not committed adultery, for William had never married her. He'd only taken her innocence and abandoned her.

"Why didn't you tell me sooner?" she demanded of her grandmother. "I—I kept searching for our marriage record, and I believed him." The rage within her rose even higher.

"I suspected the truth, but it was only recently that it was confirmed," Lady Traveston admitted. "My men found the false clergyman who 'married' you, and when I heard that the viscount had returned, I set off to tell you."

Instead of being glad to hear it, the truth hurt even more. "My son and I suffered through a hard winter in my father's cottage, after we were tossed out of Hawthorne House. You never bothered to see us then."

Her grandmother only waved a hand. "You could have traveled to London and stayed with me, if you'd wanted to. I did write you a letter. But you were too proud to humble yourself, weren't you?"

Juliana said nothing to that, for it was true. She could have taken Harry to Lady Traveston, but she'd not wanted to ask for help.

"Besides that, you were in love and as stubborn as your mother was," her grandmother continued. "I tried to warn you, but you believed every tale Hawthorne spun."

She had. At the time, she'd fallen neatly into his trap, traveling toward Scotland before they'd wed. Shame cast its pall over her, making her wish she'd never laid eyes upon William. Because of his vile tricks, her son would be ridiculed by his peers as a bastard.

"Even if I...did remarry, I'm afraid for Harry," she

admitted. "His schoolmates will tease him because of me."

"They might. But if he becomes rich enough, it won't matter in the end. Money will solve nearly any problem."

That might be true, but it would not save a tarnished name.

"Think upon it," her grandmother advised. "If you wed a respectable man, he can provide for both of you. In time, it will be forgotten."

Juliana sat upon the bed, her confidence bruised and shaken. "I will think about it."

But weighing heavier upon her mind was Grelod's earlier prediction, and she wondered if she was with child. If that came to pass, it would irreparably damage her in the eyes of every man. She would have no choice but to isolate herself and Harry.

"Oh, I nearly forgot," her grandmother said. A glint came into her eye that suggested she hadn't at all forgotten anything. "This arrived for you, along with a note from His Grace, the Duke of Somerford. It seems that he and his son have decided to return to London. I thought you might like to know, seeing how you and Lord Thorgraham are friends."

Lady Traveston passed over a folded note, along with a paper-wrapped package. It was long and narrow, and Juliana unwrapped it carefully. Her grandmother was staring at her as if a strong gaze would encourage her to hurry up.

The gift was covered in blue velvet, and when she unfolded it, she saw Arik's dagger. The blade gleamed in the light, while the wooden hilt held carvings of runes she didn't recognize.

"Now what on earth is that for?" her grandmother wondered aloud. "What does the note say?"

Juliana read the contents and bit back a laugh. She handed it over to Lady Traveston, and the scrawled words read: *He's not a girl.*

Her grandmother frowned. "I don't understand. Who isn't a girl? And why did Lord Thorgraham send you a knife? What sort of man is he?"

"It's a joke, Grandmama. And the knife is a gift for Harry."

"Now what would Harry want with that? He'll only go about stabbing things he shouldn't. Mark my words, if you let that child near a blade, he'll go and skewer himself."

Juliana wrapped up the dagger, but the moment she did, her heart stumbled. Arik was here, in London. He'd come back, in spite of everything.

For her.

"I could strangle a man with this," Arik remarked to the duke, holding up the cravat. He could not understand why any man would want to wrap his neck up like a burial shroud.

"True," Somerford remarked. "But if you wish to court Lady Hawthorne, you've no choice but to wear it."

The duke stared at him for a moment, his gaze holding regret. It was clear that troubling thoughts plagued him, though he said nothing.

"What is it?" Arik asked, fumbling with the knots.

"It bothers me that you look so much like my son. It feels as if he's been returned to me, but in a different way."

"I could say the same," he admitted, abandoning the

cravat and allowing the duke to tie it. "You look a great deal like my father did when he was alive."

The duke stood back, rubbing his chin. "So what are we to do, then? Lie to society and afterward, you'll go on your way?"

Arik crossed his arms and met the man's open gaze. "I have given you my brother's treasure. It should be enough to compensate you for this deception. When I am gone, I will take nothing from you."

The old man eyed him for a long moment. There was weariness in his gaze, along with a thread of hope. "I would give it all up for another chance to see my son. Are you certain I won't see him again?"

"Not in the way you want to see him," Arik said. But from the sadness in the old man's gaze, he wanted to offer something else. "But...sometimes I think that a part of his spirit lives on in me."

"Like the book and the tea," the duke said. There was a flare in his eyes, a hope so fierce that Arik had not the heart to take it from him.

"Yes. He was sorry for not saying good-bye to you," Arik finished. That was all he could remember, but he hoped it would give the duke peace to know it.

The man's eyes gleamed, but he gave a single nod. "Thank you for that."

Arik reached out and touched the man's shoulder, not really knowing why he did it. But he added, "If I could go back and tell my own father good-bye, this I would do. But he will never know that I regretted my anger with him. I have lost my family and everyone I ever loved."

The only person who had given him a respite from the loneliness was Juliana and her boy. He wanted to see her again, to know that she had arrived in London safely. But more than that, he wanted her to smile again, to find joy in her son.

The duke gave orders for a carriage to be brought around for them. Then he continued, "When you see Lady Hawthorne tonight, allow me to make the introductions. And whenever you meet someone I introduce you to, simply repeat the name back and bow."

Arik agreed with that advice. Repeating names was far easier than attempting to speak with strangers in a language that was not truly his own.

The duke paused a moment and added, "There is a rumor around town that Lord Hawthorne has returned from the Continent."

Interesting tidings indeed. His mood darkened at the idea of Juliana's husband trying to claim her once more—especially after William of Arthur had harmed her in the past. If he dared to touch her, Arik would tear him apart.

"Will he be there tonight?" Though he knew he was not supposed to bring weapons to this gathering, he was itching for a fight.

"I do not know. But if it is your intention to come to her aid, you should ask Lady Hawthorne what *she* wants. She may not welcome your interference."

Arik crossed his arms. "I will ensure that no one attempts to harm her."

He suspected that others might try to humiliate Juliana, if her marriage had indeed been a false one. But he intended to remain at her side, whether she wanted him there or not.

Juliana felt the stares of everyone when she entered Lady Spencer's ball. She didn't want to be here at all, though

Grandmama had demanded it of her. Especially since William had returned.

Her body was as cold as ice, her hands as frozen as her heart. This was the night she'd feared most of all—the night when she would confront her former husband at last and face down the deception. She'd been so young and foolish, not realizing how he'd taken advantage of her.

For a moment, she stood close to the wall while her grandmother greeted their hostess. A lovely woman with blond hair was standing stiffly behind her, and not a single fold of her blue gown held a wrinkle. Her gloved hands were folded, and beside her stood an even younger girl who was possibly sixteen.

"Do you think you'll find a husband tonight, Margaret?" the girl was asking. Before the woman could answer, she rolled her eyes to the ceiling and prayed in a low voice, "Please God, let someone marry my sister and take her away from the house. I would be forever grateful."

Juliana couldn't help but smile at the girl. Her older sister, however, did *not* appear amused.

"Be quiet, Amelia," she hissed. "Others will hear you."

"Oh, I do hope so." The girl winked at Juliana. "I am Amelia Andrews, and this is my sister Margaret. If you happen to know of a gentleman in need of a wife, please do feel free to introduce him to her. Margaret does prefer a man with all of his teeth, if that is possible."

Margaret Andrews sent Juliana a pained look. "Please do ignore my younger sister. She has not yet learned proper behavior, and I was forced to bring her."

Juliana only smiled. "I understand." But as she nodded in farewell to the ladies, Amelia pointed at her own teeth in a not-so-subtle reminder.

Her grandmother took her by the hand and commanded, "Stand up straight and follow me." She made all the appropriate introductions, and Juliana remembered Lady Spencer from the last time she'd met her, many years ago. It was not so difficult to fall into the familiar pattern of smiling and remaining demure while saying absolutely nothing.

When they entered the ballroom, Lady Traveston reminded her, "Do not look so bereft, Juliana. Yours is not the only scandal here." The older woman nodded toward two gentlemen scowling in the corner. "You've heard what happened to Jack Warwick, Lord Gabriel Stanhope, and Rory Fitzwalter, I presume."

Juliana shook her head, uncertain why Grandmama would bother to gossip about the three bachelors. It had to be a distraction of some form, something to keep her mind off William. "No, what happened?"

"There was a baby left on Warwick's doorstep. Fitzwalter and Lord Stanhope are staying with him, and no one knows who fathered the child. Everyone is wagering whether it was him, Fitzwalter, or Stanhope." The matron nodded toward Fitzwalter. "Personally, I believe it was *him*. If any man could tempt a woman into sinning, I'd choose Fitzwalter."

The very mention of sin brought about the vision of Arik Thorgrim and his hardened muscles. The man knew how to touch her, his hands caressing her skin in a way that tempted her to surrender. God help her, she couldn't stop thinking of the night she'd spent in his arms. Especially now.

But she forced her attention back to her grandmother's conversation. "Why does it matter who the father is?"

"Oh, it matters not a whit. But it does make the subject of a good wager." She led Juliana toward the corner.

"Then, of course, there are the foreigners. Though I can't say why on earth Lady Spencer would invite strangers from so far away. They remind me of gypsies, don't you agree? So dark and mysterious. That one over there is King Vlad, and the other man is Count Grazki. Perhaps one of them might do as a husband."

The two men appeared menacing, though their looks were striking. The king wore an ornate gold-laced military uniform in a dark burgundy shade, almost the color of dried blood. It was decorated with a sapphire order upon a white sash. His piercing blue eyes could be considered handsome, but Juliana suspected that he was a man accustomed to distancing himself from the world.

"Ah, there he is." Lady Traveston waved her fan toward the opposite side of the billiards room. "The man you've been searching for these past six years."

A wave of nausea passed over her, and Juliana gripped her fan so hard her knuckles went white. Grandmama was right. There, in the corner, was William Arthur, the man she had called husband for part of a year. She stared at him, feeling a sudden rise of fury. Her vision blurred, and she struggled to maintain a façade of calm.

"Shall I accompany you?" Lady Traveston offered. Juliana shook her head. William was hers to confront.

"No, I am fine. But I would like a moment alone to gather my thoughts."

Her grandmother appeared reluctant, but found a reason to converse with another matron nearby. Juliana stood by the wall, eying the man whose face mirrored Harry's. What on earth should she say to him? *Hello, it's been six years. We have a son now.*

No, she rather thought the viscount would give her the cut direct, humiliating her even further. It was better to take him by surprise.

"You should have brought my dagger," a deep voice said from behind her.

She turned and saw Arik Thorgrim standing there. He was dressed like a duke's son, with a black tailcoat and a snowy white cravat. His breeches were buff-colored, and they fit his body, outlining his heavy thighs. He had tied back his hair in a queue with a dark ribbon. Seeing him in these clothes made her fully aware of how handsome he was, albeit in a wild manner. And she couldn't help but smile.

"I never expected to see you again," she admitted. "Thank you for the dagger you sent. Though I still believe Harry is too young for it."

"I learned to use a dagger at the age of four," Arik said. "Harry is not at all too young."

She had her doubts on that point, but did not argue. Yet when she studied the Viking a little closer, she noticed a large bulge near his waistcoat. She leaned in and whispered, "Did you bring a dagger into Lady Spencer's ballroom?"

"No. It's a battle-ax," he clarified.

As if that was a better choice? Juliana tightened her lips, trying to hold back her amusement. "And what did you hope to do with your battle-ax?"

Arik sent her a wicked look. "Challenge the viscount to a battle. I would enjoy spilling his blood to grant you vengeance."

She grimaced at that. "I don't think that will be necessary. But I am glad you are here."

And she was. Arik's presence gave her the strength to face what lay ahead. With him, she could stand straighter, knowing that he would allow no one to speak out against her.

"You look beautiful," he said in a low voice. The

instinct rose up in her to argue that she was not at all beautiful. Her gown was the nondescript color of pastry, for there had been no time to order a new one. And yet, the look in his eyes was appreciative, causing her to hold her tongue. Then he leaned in closer, dropping his voice to a whisper. "I liked what you wore the other night even more."

Heat burned through her at his voice, and she nearly stumbled. But when he smiled at her, she felt the warmth spread through her skin and deep into her heart.

"Are you not enjoying yourself, *kjære*?" he asked. "You seem unhappy."

"I'm nervous," she admitted. "When I look at William, he makes me feel like such a fool."

Arik took her hand and started to pull her toward the dancing. "Come. We will join the others, and leave him for the moment."

Juliana held back. "But you don't know how to do these dances." She wasn't at all certain this was a wise idea. How could a Viking take part in a quadrille or one or the country dances?

"You will show me." He drew her among the other ladies and stood across from her. And though her mind was reeling at the thought of dancing with this man who had a battle-ax hidden in his waistcoat, a part of her *did* want to make William aware of what he'd lost when he'd abandoned her.

"All right," she agreed. "Then you must do as I do."

The music began, and she curtsied deeply. Arik mimicked her curtsy, bending his knees. Juliana barely held back her mirth, but she shook her head. "You're meant to bow, my lord. Like the men." But she reached out for his hand, and they stepped toward one another.

To his credit, Arik did keep up with the dancing, and more than one of the ladies eyed her with envy. Once, he spun her too quickly, and she stumbled. Before she could fall, Arik lifted her up, setting her down on the opposite line.

But when one of the gentlemen reached out to take her hand during a partner switch, Arik moved between them. "She is with me." The dark look in his eyes warned the man that he was not going to relinquish her.

His hand reached for the battle-ax, but Juliana intervened, "There is no need for that, my lord." The last thing she wanted was for him to begin fighting the other guests. As a distraction, she asked, "Would you like a glass of lemonade? Or something to eat, perhaps?" There were long tables set up with refreshments, and it was likely the best means of avoiding conflict. She also wanted more time before she faced William.

Arik eyed her as if he could read her thoughts. But he shrugged. "If you are hungry, I will join you in food and mead."

She led him away from the dancing, through the billiards room, and toward the food. When they reached the assortment, he stared at it as if he'd never seen such an array.

Likely he hasn't, a voice inside her suggested.

Juliana selected a piece of cake and put a spoonful of plum preserves beside it. "Try this," she said, offering him a plate and a fork.

Arik ignored the fork but picked up the piece of cake in his hand and ate it. The wide smile on his face provoked a desire to laugh. He dipped his finger in the plum preserves and licked it. "I like this."

"You—you're supposed to use the silver," she said. "To keep your hands clean." She glanced around to see if anyone had noticed them. It did seem that most of the bystanders had seen him use his fingers. "Didn't His Grace give you gloves to wear?"

"I did not want to wear them," he countered. Nodding toward the cake, he handed her his plate. "I will have another."

"Only if you use silver this time," she warned. "And you can try the strawberry preserves or perhaps some cream as well."

She chose another slice of cake and added strawberry preserves with a generous helping of clotted cream. Then she used the fork to slice a bit of cake, dipping it lightly in the strawberries and cream. "Try this."

Instead of eating it himself, he lifted the fork to her mouth. "You have not had anything to eat."

She had no choice but to taste it, and her cheeks reddened as she thought of all the people watching him feed her. It was quite improper, but she tasted the sweet flavor of the cake. Arik never took his eyes off her, and he was staring at her as if he wanted to kiss her in front of everyone.

Juliana handed him the plate. "Here, take this. I have to return to my grandmother."

"Have I frightened you?" he asked, beneath his breath. He caught her hand to prevent her from leaving.

The truth was, he had. Everything about this man terrified her, making her feel more deeply than she'd felt before. Emotions that had gone dormant were now reawakened.

In a low whisper, she admitted, "I'm afraid of what I feel when I look at you. I'm afraid of what everyone is saying about me now. I should not even be here."

"Have you spoken to him yet?" He switched to

Norwegian, keeping his voice low so that only she could hear.

"No. I need to, but I'm afraid of the answers I'll learn."

His palm pressed against her spine. "Then I will speak to him as your new protector."

She knew he should not touch her thusly, especially not in public. But for unknown reasons, she allowed it. He guided her away from the table of refreshments, back toward the billiards room, where she had seen William earlier.

Juliana steeled herself for the confrontation that was inevitable. All around her, she saw the gaze of the ton watching them. In their eyes, she saw their disapproving looks. They believed that she had been William's mistress, and that now she had become Arik's.

The Duke of Somerford had allowed them to think his son had returned from being lost at sea, though why he'd agreed to the deception, she didn't know. Perhaps it was because of the treasure they had given to the man. But whatever the reason, she was grateful that he had given Arik a means to be here this night.

"You've nothing to fear from your husband or anyone else," Arik said to her. "I will see to it that you and Harry have your lands and home returned to you. If he dares to speak a word against you, I'll gut him."

She did smile at that, against her will. "It might be messy if you use a battle-ax."

"I don't care." His possessive tone held a hint of violence, as if he was anticipating a fight. But she didn't want one—this was her battle to face, regardless of what he believed. "It isn't necessary for you to be involved," she said softly. "I can face him on my own. I need to."

"Then you deprive me of the joy of killing him."

Juliana turned to face him. "Why do you want to harm him? William did nothing to you."

"You don't believe me when I tell you why I was brought here. Do you think yourself unworthy of having someone to fight for you?"

"No one has ever fought for me," she admitted.

His eyes met hers, and in them, she saw an intensity that humbled her. "You are worth fighting for, Juliana. And not once have I lied to you about who I am."

She felt her defenses weakening. Right now, she wanted to rest her head against his heart and feel his strong arms around her. But she could not do anything at all. Instead, she tried to make light of her feelings, saying, "If you fight William, you'd get blood all over Lady Spencer's floor. I don't think she would appreciate that. And the servants might not want to remove a dead body."

His hand moved up her spine to the buttons of her gown. "I could kill him outside."

This time, she understood that he was indeed teasing her. She turned to look at him and saw the warmth in his eyes. "I'll think about it." She forced herself to step away from his touch, though she liked having his hands upon her.

In the Norse tongue, he murmured, "Are you well, Juliana? Has she taken care of you?"

He was referring to her grandmother, and Juliana gave a nod. "Well enough, I suppose. Though I miss Hawthorne House."

"We will return there, when this is finished." But the grimness in his voice suggested that he believed his time was running out. "And when I go, you will have all that you need to take care of your son."

"What about you?"

His expression held a hint of regret. "If the gods are willing, I will die with honor and take my rightful place in Valhalla, *kjære*."

"You won't die," she insisted. The idea of not seeing this man again bothered her more than it should. She had grown too accustomed to being with him each day.

He gave her no answer, but returned his hand to her spine. "Look, Juliana. He is watching us."

She glanced across the room and saw William staring at them. From the confused expression on his face, it was clear that he'd not expected her to be here.

Her instinct was to flee, to walk out of this ballroom and avoid the truth. But when he turned his back on her without approaching, she knew. The truth had been there all along. They had never been married. He'd seduced her and left her behind, making a mockery of her virtue. Once again, the ill feeling returned to her stomach.

"Have courage," Arik said. "Come." He gripped her hand, leaving her no means of escaping this. The people of the ton were watching them, waiting to see how this scandal would unfold. But before they could reach William, Marcus stepped forward.

"Miss Nelson," he interrupted. "I know that you believe my brother has wronged you. But I would ask that if you wish to speak with him, that you do so in private. Not here."

She agreed with that, but Arik pressed her behind him. "You are the man who forced Juliana and her son to leave Hawthorne House." He spoke the words with a thinly veiled anger. Marcus eyed him, then Juliana.

"Lord Thorgraham, it has been many years since we've met. I am glad that you have safely returned to England." Marcus extended his hand, but Arik ignored it.

Instead, he stared down at the man, his eyes holding coldness. "What kind of a man forces a woman and child out of their home?"

"I allowed them to stay for six years," Marcus answered calmly. "It was not a decision I made lightly, I assure you. She and her son had no right to be there."

Juliana stared back at the man. "Did you know that William was alive? And that he tricked me into a false marriage?"

Marcus stiffened. "I will not speak ill of my brother. But yes, I suspected as much. He has been known to do as he pleases. As for whether he was alive, no, I could not be certain until I saw him with my own eyes."

The haughty tone in his voice made her aware that the man hadn't actually wanted his brother to return. Undoubtedly, the estates were under better care beneath Marcus's guidance.

"William never wrote to anyone in all those years," he continued. "I suspected he was unable to travel back to England, owing to the war."

"If you knew that he never married me, why did you wait so long to make us leave?" It startled her to realize that this man was not the villain she'd made him out to be. The true villain was across the billiards room, flirting with a young debutante.

"I did not know it for certain until recently." He met Juliana's gaze and answered, "But you remained far away from London society, and you were wise enough to keep to yourself. As you said, what kind of man would force a woman and child out of their home? I had no choice, once I became engaged to Miss Whitemore, for she would not approve of another mistress in residence at Hawthorne House."

Juliana's throat tightened with emotion, and she now

understood that Marcus had been more than lenient with them. He might be a cold-hearted man who rarely spoke with kindness, but he could have forced them to leave far sooner—especially since she had never married his brother.

She sighed and admitted, "Let him be, Arik. William bears the blame."

Her Viking stared hard at Marcus and pushed his way past the man. He reached beneath his waistcoat for the battle-ax, revealing the deadly blade as he crossed through the billiards room.

Oh dear. This was not going to go well.

Juliana hurried forward. "Arik, not here. Not in this place."

But he ignored her and went to stand directly in front of William. Seeing him again brought back all her feelings of insecurity. Of how he'd kept her hidden from the rest of London at Hawthorne House. How he'd visited her a few times, only to take her to bed and teach her what he wanted.

Humiliation burned through her cheeks, but she forced herself to stand before him. "You've been gone for many years, William. I thought you might have sent word that you'd returned to England."

He didn't look at her at all, his attention focused on Arik. There was a flash of fear in his eyes when he spied the battle-ax. "Lord Thorgraham, I believe."

His utter disregard for her, as if she were invisible, was a blow she should have expected. But it hurt to know that her worst fears were true—that he had never cared at all for her. That he'd used and discarded her.

The rage in Arik's eyes was staggering. He looked as if he was ready to take off William's head with the weapon. Instead, he spoke only two words. "Outside. Now."

"Is there a problem, Thorgraham? You seem rather upset about something."

She could hardly believe what he'd said. Upset? As if she were nothing but an afterthought? And what of their son? She had written letters to him, telling him of her pregnancy. Had he ever received them?

Arik took a step forward, staring down at the man. "You abandoned Juliana and your son, leaving them barely able to survive. It does make me angry, yes."

His tone was so calm, it held an edge like a dagger's blade. And worse, Lord Hawthorne didn't even react to the news of Harry. Instead, he met Arik's gaze openly. "I don't believe you have anything to do with this. Miss Nelson and I were acquainted for a time—"

"Don't you mean your *wife*?" Arik corrected.

At that, William risked a glance toward her. He shrugged and admitted, "That was simply a farce. She was a fetching young girl, several years ago. Even so, I would never stoop to wed a fisherman's daughter—even if her mother was once the daughter of a baron." He shrugged, not even deigning to look at her. "Juliana and I had our bit of fun. It was never serious."

A hot flash of anger swept over her. Never serious? She'd given up years of her life waiting for this man, remaining true to him. She had raised their son and had let Harry believe that one day his father might return. And yet William intended to turn his back on them?

Murder was too good for the man. His betrayal affected not only her own future, but also that of their son. Her maternal protective instincts were raging with the full-fledged need for vengeance. He could not walk away from them without providing for Harry.

Juliana stepped forward and said, "Our marriage was serious to me. And I agree with Lord Thorgraham. We should take this discussion elsewhere." Before she seized the battle-ax from Arik and used it to release her own frustration.

"I'm not going anywhere," William argued.

At that, Arik seized the man by his cravat, half choking him. He lifted the man off the ground and began dragging him outside the billiards room. There were audible gasps from the onlookers, and Juliana didn't doubt that this scandal would be talked about for the rest of the night.

Was it bad that she found it gratifying to see her so-called husband hauled away like a sack of grain? Really, he deserved it.

She followed them out of the room, and Arik continued pulling William by his cravat, as if it were a dog's leash. The footman opened the door for them, and soon enough, they were standing on the stone steps.

"I say, Thorgraham, what's got into you? She was my mistress, nothing more, and not a very good one at that."

Juliana saw the clench of Arik's jaw and took a step backward. He hadn't released William, but he was studying the man as if determining how he wanted to kill him.

"I suppose she's your paramour now," William remarked. "But you've no reason to concern yourself with me. I finished with her a long time ago, and you are welcome to her."

Arik slowly tightened his grip around the man's cravat until William began turning purple. As her former husband began grasping at his throat, clawing for air, Juliana stepped forward. "I cannot believe I wasted so much of my life with a man like you. You deceived me with our marriage and left me to believe you were dead."

"I could make that happen," Arik suggested.

It was more tempting than she wanted to admit. But instead, she shook her head. "Let him go."

He released his hold on the man, and William staggered to his knees, gasping for air. There was no mercy in Arik's eyes as he stared down at the man. "You will provide for Juliana and your son. Enough that they will live their lives in comfort."

"I have no son," Hawthorne gasped. "If she bore a child, he's not mine. I owe her nothing."

She couldn't speak a word, for his denial wounded her in a way she'd never expected. Harry was an innocent boy who had never harmed anyone. His eager nature brought joy into her life, and he did not deserve to be ignored by his father or treated as a bastard. Her anger was staggering, and she clenched her fists, struggling to control the rage.

"He is a child of your blood, and you will not cast him aside," she insisted. "He deserves the life he should have had."

"He'll get nothing from me," William remarked. "Not a bloody farthing."

She swung out her fist and connected with his jaw. The blow hurt her hand, but before William could strike her in retaliation, Arik caught the man's hand. "I should break all the bones in this hand, for what you did to her."

Her rage was not merely for the way William had nearly hit her—it was also for the way he'd broken her during the months of their marriage, making her believe that she was not good enough for him.

"You will give her the lands and the dwelling at Hawthorne House," Arik demanded, tightening his grip.

William let out a cry of pain, struggling to free himself. "The lands are entailed," he argued. "Neither she, nor her bastard, can have them."

At that, Arik's face remained impassive. His knuckles whitened, and William screamed, grasping his hand in agony as if his bones were indeed breaking beneath the force of the Viking's grip.

She supposed she ought to pity him or urge Arik to stop. Instead, she took satisfaction in watching William suffer. He deserved it for what he'd done.

At that moment, Marcus opened the door and hurried outside to join them. A pained expression came over his face when he saw his brother. When Arik released William, the man writhed on the ground, clutching his hand.

Marcus kept a visible distance and addressed him. "Lord Thorgraham, I understand that you have become Miss Nelson's...*protector*. But it would be better to discuss this in a civil manner. Tomorrow morning, you will both come to my town house. I will see what arrangements can be made to offer compensation to Miss Nelson for my brother's...indiscretion."

An indiscretion? It was far worse than that. Lord Hawthorne had ruined her in the eyes of everyone and had taken her dignity. No amount of money would atone for that.

But when Juliana studied Marcus's face, she saw regret and embarrassment in his eyes. It did seem that he was trying to help them, though she wasn't certain she wanted anything from him.

William staggered to his feet and shot his brother a furious look. "Let Thorgraham provide for her and the bastard. If he wants her, the money won't matter to him."

Before Juliana could react, Arik's fist connected with William's jaw. The man reeled and dropped to the ground like a brick.

Marcus stood there, looking uncomfortable. "I cannot

say he didn't deserve that." Then he took a step backward. "Lord Thorgraham, please accept my apologies for my brother's actions. I will attempt to make things right on his behalf. But since I am not in command of the estates any longer, there is not a great deal I can do."

Juliana realized that Marcus was hardly concerned about her welfare; he seemed more worried about offending a duke's son. There was far greater social damage if their family offended the Duke of Somerford.

She gave a nod to show him that she'd heard his words. Yet inside, she felt hollow, as if her life had collapsed upon itself. William hadn't wanted anything to do with her or with their son. Now, she wished she'd never seen him again.

"I want to go home," she told Arik.

"Then I will take you there." He guided her up the stairs and inside the doors. "Wait here until I return."

She ordered the footman to bring the carriage around and tell her grandmother that she was leaving early. Numbly, she leaned against the wall, wishing she could disappear. No one spoke to her, though she knew they were gossiping. When Arik returned, he was holding a white cloth napkin with something folded inside.

"I've already sent for my grandmother's carriage," she told him. "I'll be all right. You needn't come with me."

"I will not let you go alone." His bearing revealed that he meant every word. Juliana decided it was best to say nothing and let him escort her. What did it matter? She had already lost her reputation and learned that she'd been deceived by the man she had once called her husband.

She wanted to weep.

Arik led her outside again and helped Juliana into the

carriage. Thankfully, William was already gone. Then her Viking joined her in the vehicle, closing the door behind him.

She said nothing, feeling the weight of her folly. Inside, she felt bruised and broken, so angry with herself. For years, she'd waited for her husband to return. Though she'd not been happy with the marriage, the gift of her son was a miracle in itself. And now Harry's life would be shadowed by the shame of illegitimacy.

"I brought cake," Arik said, unfolding the napkin. The moment he did, her tears started to fall. It was such a thoughtful gesture that it broke apart the fragile hold upon her feelings. She wept for the foolish dreams she'd had, that somehow William would acknowledge their marriage. Even if the worst happened, if he'd wanted to divorce her, she could have protected Harry's inheritance. Now, they had nothing at all. Not even her good name.

Arik set the cake aside and drew her into his lap, holding her close. She cried until his shirt was damp from her tears, but she didn't care. He said nothing but stroked her back while she wept.

"I should have killed him," he said, matter-of-factly. "He deserved to die."

Juliana sniffled, "I'm glad you didn't. I wouldn't want you to hang for murder." She drew back to look at him, knowing that she was likely a pitiful mess. But from the way he was looking at her, he didn't seem to care.

"I will still fight for you and your son," he said, resting his hand upon the base of her neck. His palm warmed her skin, and she grew sensitive to his touch, reminded of the desire he'd kindled.

"I never should have believed a word he said," she admitted, feeling the embarrassment rising within her. "I should have known that he would do something like that, in order to seduce me."

And then, what William had said about her...that she'd not been any good...it made her even angrier.

Arik's thumb grazed the pulse point at her throat, and she grew aware of his desire, for she was seated upon his lap. Though he didn't speak, there was no doubting that he wanted her.

"He was unworthy of you, *kjære*. You are better off without him."

"I am a fallen woman now," she admitted. "I bore a son to a man who was not my husband."

"It was not your fault," he insisted. "In the eyes of the gods, there was no shame. You spoke your vows, believing them. That is all that matters."

"But Harry will suffer for it. They will taunt him."

"Then I will teach him to fight his enemies. No one will taunt him."

She almost smiled, for she believed he would. Any man who would give a knife as a gift would undoubtedly teach her son how to defend himself. But she said softly, "You told me you would not be here when the moon has ended its phases."

His expression darkened, and he reached around her waist with both hands. "I cannot say how much longer I have, Juliana of Arthur."

Inside, she held a deep fear that he would be gone within a matter of days. And she didn't want that—not at all.

The carriage came to a stop in front of her grandmother's home, and she suddenly realized that she could not bring Arik inside. He would have to leave her here...and that wasn't what she wanted.

With trembling hands, she touched his face. "I gave

everything of myself to William, and he gave me only shame in return. I'm angry at the choices I made and all the years I lost." Her heart was aching with grief and needs she didn't understand. "Take me back to where you are staying. This night, I would rather be with you."

His gaze held a hunger that echoed her own. Briefly, he opened the door and spoke to the driver, giving the order to return to the duke's town house. When he returned to her, he said, "I'm going to spend all night pleasuring you, *kjære*. And when I've finished, you won't remember any man but me."

ChAPTER EIGHT

Arik guided Juliana up the steps of the house, but her face was pale with fear. She kept her gaze averted, and he opened the door for her. A footman hurried forward, but Arik waved him back.

"Can I get you anything, my lord? Shall I send a maid to prepare your room?"

He shook his head. "I will take care of it myself. Leave us." The footman obeyed, and Arik led Juliana up another staircase toward the room the Duke of Somerford had given him.

She hadn't spoken a single word since they'd left the carriage, and it made him tense to see the lingering hurt in her eyes. She had been faithful to a man who had betrayed her, and now her son would bear the shame. He understood how it felt to be made into a fool.

Svala and Eyker had deceived him in the same way, filling him with such wrath that he'd attacked Eyker without thinking. His reaction had cost him his life, and he didn't know how much longer he could stay in this world. But he would not rest until William of Arthur had compensated Juliana for what he'd done.

Once they were inside his bedchamber, Arik built a

fire upon the hearth. When a warm blaze had started, Juliana came to stand before it, holding her gloved hands out. Her hair was still bound up, and a strand of pearls rested at her throat.

"I shouldn't be here," she murmured. "I know what others will say about me."

"I care not for anything they say. The only one I care for is standing before me." He moved in closer. Juliana's eyes were red from crying, and she looked weary of the world.

She raised her eyes to his, and in them, he saw desolation and fear. "I never thought my life would turn out this way." Her hands were knotted together and she added, "I tried to do everything right. I chose a nobleman, and I thought I had married him. I tried to be a good wife to him and bore him a son. But in the end, he left me with nothing."

He rested his palm against her cheek, caressing the soft skin. Then he picked up her hand and drew it around his neck. "You are not alone, *kjære*." Despite the tumultuous few days, he wanted her to know that. He would fight for her until his life ceased to exist.

Juliana stared at him with those troubled gray eyes, as if she knew not what to do anymore. "I am glad you are here." She leaned in, resting her cheek against his.

Her words slid around him like an embrace, making him realize that he had never cared for Svala in this way. Juliana was a woman of courage, a woman any man would be proud to love. Yet, a coldness filled him at the realization that he could not stay.

Already, he was losing feeling in his feet and lower legs. It was a strange sensation, to walk as a normal man did, but not to feel a single step. He sensed it was a sign from the gods, that he had only a few days remaining. On the last day, he would feel nothing at all. And though he'd expected that all of this would end, it was a chilling reminder that his time was running out.

He'd believed these weeks had been a second chance, a way of earning a place for himself in the afterworld. Now, he wondered if they were a punishment. He had met a woman of honor whom he did not want to leave behind. But he had no right to remain in her world. He had already died once, and his time here was fleeting.

He kissed her softly. "Before I leave, I will see to it that you have your vengeance."

She never broke her gaze with his, but her hands crossed over her waist, like a woman who was with child. It was an unconscious gesture, but it did make him wonder what it would have been like to sire a child with Juliana. She was exactly the sort of woman he might have once wed.

"I am glad you struck William down." Her voice held traces of fury. "And I wish I had known about William's deception sooner. I *was* faithful to him all those years. At least, until you came."

"And now?" He reached for her waist, resting his hands at her hips.

"I feel lost inside. I don't know what to do…where to go." She shook her head, resting her hands upon his. Then she lifted her chin. "I just needed to be away from all of it tonight," she admitted.

"You may stay as long as you want." Never would he turn her away.

"Thank you." Juliana tried to muster a smile, but her pale complexion belied her words. Whatever the reason she'd come here this night, it seemed that her courage was faltering. "Why did the duke bring you with him to London? Why is he allowing you to pose as his son?"

"I did give him half of my brother's fortune," he said. But he knew it was more than that. The older man watched him as if he half-expected Arik to somehow transform back into his lost son. "And the lie gave me a means of seeing you again. Others believe I am his son."

"You do look like him," Juliana admitted. She added, "I should warn you...since they believe you are a marquess, every woman in London will throw herself at you."

"I will not be here for long," he said. "And there is only one woman I want."

Her face held a blush, and she shrugged. "Thank you for being here. I am grateful for everything."

He traced a line down her jaw while he took in the beauty of her face, the golden hair and her gray eyes holding back the storm of her emotions. There was a faint tingle in his fingertips, as if to warn him that he would soon lose feeling in his hands. "What do you need from me this night?" he asked. "Whatever that may be, I will give it."

"I want something for myself," she admitted. "A night in your arms."

He understood that she wanted to lose herself in physical release, to push away the hurt that she'd endured.

"Kiss me," he commanded, wanting her to make the first move. She closed the distance, rising on tiptoe, lifting her mouth to his. He tasted the salt of her earlier tears and the desperation.

But this night, he would turn her sadness into pleasure. He reached behind her, fumbling with the cursed buttons. He preferred the ties that women wore in his time, for it was far easier to get them naked. After jerking at the buttons, still kissing her, Juliana started to laugh against his mouth. "You don't need to rip off the buttons, Arik. Just push them through the holes." The amusement on her face was better than her earlier disappointment.

After he managed to unfasten the gown, he lifted it over her head, revealing another layer. The white linen was gathered into tucks and embroidered with rose thread. Someone had spent a great deal of time making the garment. Juliana's arms were bare and it exposed a large expanse of her throat and the skin above her breasts.

"I am beginning to see why you required a servant to help you undress." He wished he could simply slit it open with a blade and be done with it. But he loosened the laces of her undergarment, turning her to face him.

She stood, her gray eyes meeting his with longing. He stopped undressing her and kissed her temple, then her jaw. He used his mouth to tempt her into surrendering herself and was rewarded when she wrapped her arms around his neck.

"I have never met a woman like you before," he admitted. "You are not of this earth. Perhaps Freya herself was your mother."

Juliana began pulling the pins from her hair, letting it fall below her shoulders. The golden mass shone in the firelight, and she reached out to untie the cravat at his neck. He removed his coat and let her lift away his shirt until he was bared before her.

"I remember the first night I was with you," she murmured, running her hands over his chest. "You were so hard. So strong."

Her words were a caress, and he caught his breath when she moved her hands over his ribs. She aroused him deeply, until all he could think of was pressing her against the wall and taking her.

He removed the garment that she'd called a corset

until she stood in only a single shift. Beneath the thin linen, he saw the darkened hue of her nipples. He wanted to taste them, to draw her into his mouth until they puckered with her own needs.

He sat down on a low stool and brought her to sit on his lap, with both of her legs around him. His rigid arousal was pressed between her legs, and she gave a slight gasp when he pulled her hips forward. The shift moved up to her waist, leaving her bare beneath. With one hand, he reached between them, feeling the soft hair of her mound.

Her fingers dug into his shoulders, and she closed her eyes. With one hand he teased her, while he pulled down her shift to reveal her bare breast. It was round and full, with a darker nipple. He bent down with his mouth, tonguing her throat. Then he slowly slipped a single finger inside her.

She let out a soft gasp, and he felt her wetness coating him. She desired him as badly as he wanted her. But he was intent on making this night one she would not forget. For time was slipping away from him.

He continued kissing a path downward, toward her breast. "Do you feel me inside you?" he murmured. To emphasize his question, he invaded her flesh, moving his finger in and out.

"Y-yes," she answered. She was holding fast to his shoulders, her head arching backward.

"Squeeze against me," he ordered.

A moment later, he felt her walls tightening. She shuddered and he rewarded her by taking her nipple into his mouth. He added a second finger inside her, and she cried out, still squeezing against him.

"Don't stop," he ordered.

Juliana couldn't have stopped if she'd wanted to. The shocking sensation of his fingers inside her was making her body ache. And then, oh then, his thumb nudged her hooded flesh like he'd done the other night. He pressed against her, circling while his tongue did the same. She strained against him, her breathing hitched, while she clenched his fingers.

The throbbing became a deep pulse that robbed her of all senses. She was drowning in sensation, feeling as if every inch of her skin was flooded with desire. Like an invading warrior, he took her under, making her tremble with the force of his touch.

She couldn't stop the wave of release that shuddered through her, sparking such a deep spasm that every inch of her skin seemed to shudder beneath his hands. It was breathtaking to be touched by this Viking.

But she didn't want to sit on his lap and accept his touches, giving nothing in return. Juliana bent down, kissing his hair and drawing him up to take his mouth with hers. She kissed him hard, slipping her tongue inside to mingle with his. Her sudden aggression pushed him even farther, and he stood up, taking her off his lap. In one swift movement, he tore her chemise down the middle. His face was harsh, offering no respite.

And she wanted none. Boldly, she reached for his trousers and began unbuttoning them, helping to rid him of his own clothing. When she finally saw his naked body, a flush came over her.

This man was not a duke's son. There was no trace of softness upon him—only ridged muscles that outlined his form. Numerous scars lined his ribs and she saw another that cut across his shoulder. Men in her time did not fight like this. They rode horses, gambled at White's, and sat in Parliament. They did not bear the scars of a man who had fought for his life.

She lowered her mouth to his chest, kissing a path over his hardened stomach. He was so different from William that merely touching him brought her a sense of wonder. It made her feel good to run her hands over him and watch his expression transform.

Arik lifted her into his arms, carrying her toward his bed. When he lay her down upon it, he covered her body with his own. Skin to skin, he kissed her, and she parted her legs so that he could move even closer.

The hard length of his erection rubbed against her, and she guided him inside her, needing to be filled by him. The moment he thrust deeply inside, he groaned, balancing his weight on his arms.

"By the gods, Juliana." He couldn't seem to form a coherent thought as she wrapped her legs around him, urging him deeper.

Slowly, he found a rhythm, sinking and withdrawing while she watched his dark eyes. "You are a Viking," she murmured. "And you are mine."

He took her nipple in his mouth, suckling her as he continued to thrust against her. In answer to his delicious torment, she squeezed him within her depths. It only deepened her own pleasure as he penetrated over and over.

"No man will ever make you feel this way," he said, holding her hips as he continued the swift rhythm. It made her imagine what it would be like if she were a Viking maiden and Arik had come for her.

God above, he knew how to seduce her. She indulged in a forbidden fantasy, letting her imagination tempt her with visions of this man. If he returned from a raid and if she was at home waiting for him, what would it be like? Would he tear her gown the way he'd torn her chemise? Would he kiss her senseless, touching her bare skin until she was desperate to have him inside her?

She clenched his length as he slid in and out, and her nipples tightened as she let the vision spin off wildly. He was lifting her hips now, and the new angle brought a new pressure within her, making it difficult to catch her breath.

"Take me," she commanded, "the way you would have, if you had found me on one of your raids." She didn't want tenderness now—this was about forgetting the world and everything in it. She wanted raw, physical lovemaking that would drive out the pain and uncertainty of her future.

"I don't rape women, *kjære*." He withdrew from her body, and she suddenly wished she hadn't spoken. That wasn't what she had meant at all.

"Forget what I said. I was just…imagining what it would be to surrender to you."

His expression turned curious, and he asked, "You want me to claim you, then."

"Yes," she whispered.

His warm hands turned her over on the bed, her backside facing him. He guided her to spread her legs apart, but he didn't take her right away. Instead, he massaged her bottom, parting her intimately so that she was breathless with anticipation. With his fingers, he grazed her wet entrance, opening her and sliding the tip of his erection inside.

Without warning, he slammed inside her core, and she muffled her scream of pleasure against the coverlet. It sent her spiraling over the edge as he drove himself against her. The sensation of being made love to like this was savage, breaking apart her inhibitions. She lost sight of who she was, becoming a woman who backed against him, nearly sobbing as he thrust again and again. With both hands, he palmed her breasts, teasing the nipples.

She was broken apart, a mindless abyss of lust and frantic need. God help her, this was what she'd wanted when she'd asked him not to leave her. Arik continued his ruthless penetrations, forcing her to come apart again.

But there was no sense of violence in his lovemaking. Instead, it was a desperation, as if he couldn't get enough of her. She trembled against him, her fists seizing the coverlet while he claimed her.

And at last, he buried himself deep inside, his rough breathing revealing that he'd found his own release. He shuddered, turning her to her side so that he had her body cradled against him. An aftershock claimed her, and she bucked against him, keeping his hands upon her breasts.

His warm body was against hers, their skin slick with sweat. She said nothing, but the shutters at the window were open, revealing the bright moon. There was only the faintest shadow upon it, and she realized that the full moon would come in another day or so.

She closed her eyes, praying that time would not separate them now.

Arik had barely slept at all last night. Having Juliana beside him had given him comfort in a way he'd never expected it to. It had felt right holding her near.

After the night they'd spent together, Juliana had asked him to escort her home. He had joined her in the carriage, and they'd spent a moment alone, driving through the London streets. His mind envisioned all the ways he wanted to touch her again, to drive her wild with abandon.

But today, he had lost sensation in his hands and fingers. There was no feeling in his legs anymore, and when he glanced at the morning sky, the moon was nearly full. He sensed that his last moments were slipping away.

Juliana was wearing the gown she'd had on the night before, and her hair was pinned up. Although outwardly she appeared composed, he could see the churn of emotions in her eyes.

"I don't regret the choices I made last night," she admitted, when they drew near to her grandmother's house, "but I worry about the consequences." Her hands rested upon her middle, and the sudden look in her eyes made him guess the reason.

"Are you with child?" he guessed. The thought warmed him with the promise of new life. A part of him would live on, and Juliana would not forget him.

She shook her head and shrugged. "It's too soon to know. But...yes, it is possible, since we spent that first night together." Her face flushed, and she asked, "Can you not stay with me?"

Though a child might indeed bind him to her, the loss of feeling in his body suggested that he could not. "I do not know," was all he could answer.

"Grandmama has spoken of me marrying again, perhaps a foreign nobleman," she confessed. "If there is a child, then I will have no choice."

A fierce jealousy caught him in the gut at the thought of another man claiming her. Juliana had given herself to *him*. He wanted no other man to have her. *At least, not while I am still breathing,* he thought.

"You need not marry again," he told her. "I will find a

way to provide for you. You deserve compensation, and that you will have."

"Or Harry and I could return to my father's house," she said. "It might be cold in the winter, but at least we have a home there. And no one will talk about the scandals I always seem to be entangled within." Her cheeks were red, as if she was embarrassed about all that had happened.

He reached out to take her hand. "Do not fear what others might say. Their words mean nothing."

That made her smile, though he suspected she believed he was teasing. The truth was, he would gladly cut down any man or woman who dared to insult her.

"I am glad you are here, Arik Thorgrim," she told him, reaching for his hand. "And if there is a child, I will take care of it. You needn't worry."

He closed his fingers around hers, but it bothered him that he could no longer feel the heat of her palm. He thought of telling her about it, but it would only cause her greater worry. Instead, he leaned in and kissed her hard. At least he could feel the softness of her lips, drinking in the taste of her. And it was enough for now.

"I have to go back inside and face my grandmother," she said. "Lady Traveston will not like what I've done."

"You will not face her alone." Though he suspected the older woman would disapprove, perhaps he could find a means of appeasing her. Particularly if she believed he was the duke's son.

The footman opened their carriage door, and Arik stepped out first, reaching up to help her down. He took a moment to memorize her features, suspecting that this was the last day he would ever see her.

"Miss Nelson," the footman interrupted, "I am glad that you've arrived. Lord Hawthorne is here."

"For what reason?" Juliana wondered aloud.

Arik didn't mind at all. He wanted to confront William of Arthur again, especially now. He touched her spine, guiding her inside. But she stopped at the steps. "Do not go with me. No good can come of this."

"You are wrong. It was for this reason that I was sent here. He must make amends for the way he wronged you."

"And he will," she said. "But I will not bring violence around my grandmother and my son. Harry adores you. What will he think if he sees you attack his father?"

Arik ignored her words. "How do you know William is not here to claim his son and take him away?"

She went utterly pale. "H-he wouldn't do that. He doesn't even know the boy. And he said last night that he doesn't care about him."

"Then why is he here this early in the morning?" Arik was uncertain of the man's purpose, but he was not about to leave them undefended.

"I don't know. But I do know that I want him nowhere near Harry." She was already hurrying forward, no longer seeming to care if he accompanied her or not. Arik kept a short distance behind her, allowing Juliana to take the lead. She paid no heed to the butler, who was trying to speak to her, but instead took the steps two at a time. It was clear that she was trying to ensure her son's safety, above all else.

He didn't follow her. Instead, he held back, waiting to catch a glimpse of William of Arthur. Something had caused the man to return here. And whether it was for Juliana or for her son, Arik intended to guard them both.

No matter what the cost.

Harry was still in his room, while the dog was asleep by the hearth.

Juliana breathed a sigh of relief, resisting the urge to snatch her son into her arms. "Good morning," she said, kissing his tousled blond hair. He hugged her and then said, "Mrs. Haverford said that my papa is here, but he doesn't want to see me. Why not?"

She took her son's hand, wishing the housekeeper had said nothing to Harry. "I don't know why, Harry. But you are a good boy, and you mustn't worry about him. Tomorrow we will leave London and go home."

He shrugged. "Will Mr. Thorgrim be there? I want him to teach me how to use my knife." It was then that Juliana realized that he'd put a sock around the blade like a sheath, and he'd tied it to his waist with a bit of string.

Her heart bled to think that his own father was downstairs, pretending as if the boy didn't exist...and Harry didn't seem to mind at all. He was more interested in Arik Thorgrim, a man he'd known hardly a fortnight.

"I don't know," she hedged. "He might come with us. He's downstairs right now." Arik had said that he would be gone when the moon was full again. She refused to let herself believe that he would go, though he'd said it. After a night in his arms, she wanted to start her life over again, spending time with a man who cared for her. He was strong and bold, a man who would stand up to anyone and damn the consequences.

"I want to see Mr. Thorgrim." Harry brightened and gripped the hilt of his dagger. "I have to show him my knife."

Juliana cursed herself for telling her son that he was

downstairs. She shouldn't have told him that. "Not yet. I must speak with your father first."

"But why?" He started toward the door, but she blocked his path.

"Wait here, and perhaps I'll send Mr. Thorgrim upstairs. You can show him your knife then." She didn't want Harry anywhere near William. Though she didn't know why her former husband was here, she wouldn't put it past him to use Harry to his own advantage.

"Do you promise?" Harry took a step back, and she nodded.

"I promise, when I have finished speaking with Lord Hawthorne, I will bring Mr. Thorgrim upstairs. Just stay here and wait for him."

Her son sighed and returned to playing with his tin soldiers. *Thank goodness.*

Juliana bid him farewell and closed the door to the nursery. She walked down the hall and spied one of Lady Traveston's maids. "Is my grandmother abed?" she asked the young woman in a low whisper.

"Yes, miss. She is suffering from one of her headaches and has asked not to be disturbed until the afternoon."

That was good. At least Juliana wouldn't have to face further questioning from her grandmother. She thanked the maid and continued down the stairs, only to find William waiting for her outside the parlor. The butler sent her a questioning look, but she dismissed him with a hand. Undoubtedly Lord Hawthorne was here to stir up trouble, and she preferred that the servants should not overhear their conversation.

There was no sign of Arik, which made her wonder if he'd left. It wasn't like him at all. But then she spied him at the far end of the hall, watching over her. Her shoulders lowered with relief, knowing that he was here to ensure that nothing happened to them.

It didn't seem that William was aware of the Viking's presence, and she approached the parlor, feeling relieved by it.

"William." She greeted him as if he were an acquaintance instead of her lost husband. "I am surprised to see you."

"I spoke with my brother last night," he said, walking toward the stairs. "And I learned that you spent several years at Hawthorne House."

"I did, yes." *Because I believed we were married and that I was your viscountess,* she thought. "Marcus allowed us to stay when we didn't know where you were."

He eyed her, his gaze narrowed. "I also heard that Lord Thorgraham gave his father half a treasure in gold and silver. Gold that was buried upon my land."

Though he spoke in a calm voice, she didn't miss the note of greed in his tone. She didn't know whether to be upset or relieved. He wasn't here about Harry—he was here about money.

She should have expected that they were worth nothing at all to him.

"It was a Viking hoard that we found on the Duke of Somerford's land, not yours," she corrected. "Thorgrim—that is, Lord Thorgraham—found it and gave it over to his...father." It was somewhat a lie, but she didn't know what else to say.

"I don't believe you." His expression hardened and he added, "And you were trespassing on my estate, long after you should have left." His tone grew silken. "Perhaps you stole other things that belonged to me."

Anger flared up inside her at his insinuation. How did

he dare accuse her of theft? "You were the one who stole from me," she countered. "You stole my dignity, and you stole my innocence."

"Oh come now, Juliana. What other titled gentleman would have had you? You should count yourself fortunate that I gave you my attentions for a time. I certainly gave you a better life than you would have had as a fisherman's daughter." He looked down at her with disdain. It was clear that he believed himself better than her.

He crossed his arms and said, "I know you kept back some of the gold for yourself. And I want my portion."

Of course he did. Because men like William believed that they deserved more than they had. "First of all, you are mistaken. I have no gold. And even if I did, the last person I would give it to is you." No longer would she obey him meekly, like a frightened eighteen-year-old girl. She had a son to protect and a life of her own—one that was better without him.

A thin smile spread over his face, and he lowered his voice. "And what if I decided to claim your boy as my bastard? I could easily arrange it so you'd never see him again."

Fury ripped through her at his threat. If he dared to threaten Harry, she would eviscerate him. "You will *never* threaten my son," she said. "Leave my grandmother's house this instant."

He reached out to seize her arm. "I don't take orders from a woman, Juliana. Especially you."

Juliana tried to wrench herself free of the man's grasp. "I asked you to leave."

At that, Arik strode closer. His arms were crossed and his mouth was tight with anger. Though he was still wearing a nobleman's clothes, she saw him reaching for a hidden weapon. The look in his eyes held violence, as if he intended to kill William for touching her.

But before he reached him, she saw Harry hurrying down the stairs. "Let go of my mother." He glared at William and rested his hand upon the blade Arik had given him, still sheathed in the sock.

She sent a pleading look toward Arik, who closed the distance and used his height to intimidate Lord Hawthorne. "The boy is right. Let go of her, before I break your arms." His voice was quiet but held the confident air of a man who kept his promises.

"Lord Thorgraham," William greeted him. "I see that you've been enjoying Juliana's charms while I was away. Like many gentlemen, I'd wager."

He made it sound as if she'd sold herself on the streets. How could she have ever been charmed by this man? It made her physically ill to think of the nights he'd shared her bed. He had reveled in dominating her, believing that he was a lover of great skill. The truth was, he'd only used and discarded her.

Hatred slid over Juliana, and she finally wrenched herself free of his grasp. William barely spared her any notice at all. The smug expression on his face made her long to strike him down. All the years of frustration and helplessness flooded through her. He'd always looked down on her, never believing that she was worth anything at all.

"And I presume this is your bastard?" Her former husband nodded toward Harry, as he released her arm. "The one you claim is mine."

Harry appeared confused and uneasy. Juliana couldn't blame him, for this was the first time he'd ever laid eyes upon his father.

"There is only one bastard here," Arik said, "and it is not the child."

The viscount lifted his gaze to the Viking, and a trace of uneasiness crossed his face. *Good*, Juliana thought. He ought to be afraid of Arik. "I have no disagreement with you, Thorgraham," William said. "I came only to speak with Juliana."

"And I warned you not to bother her again." Her Viking seized William's arm, his hand still gripping the handle of his battle-ax. "You hold no claim upon her."

"Take her," her former husband insisted. "She's nothing to me and never was. All I want is my share of the gold." He tried to pull back but could not free himself from Arik's grasp. "Let go of me."

There was not a trace of mercy upon the Viking's face. "Come near her or the boy again, and I will kill you." His voice was low, but his words held an unbreakable vow.

A sudden flicker of distaste passed over William's face. "I said, let me go, Thorgraham." The viscount reached into his coat pocket and withdrew a small flintlock pistol. He pressed the barrel toward Arik's throat. "I will not be treated like this."

Juliana froze in place, uncertain of whether it was an idle threat. Her Viking didn't appear at all concerned, no doubt because he'd never seen a pistol before.

"Am I supposed to be afraid?" He stared back at William as if he were nothing more than an irritating insect.

"Be careful, Arik," she warned. Though she didn't truly think William would fire the weapon, a sudden premonition ripped through her that he was going to die. Hadn't Arik said that he would only be here until the moon grew full? The cold fear settled over her, and she tried to regain command of herself.

"I will use this, if you don't let me go," William insisted. "I swear I will."

"No, don't shoot! Leave Mr. Thorgrim alone!" Her son rushed forward, and unsheathed the knife, as if to defend Arik.

No. Not Harry.

Juliana watched in horror as the boy lifted the blade. In that split second, she saw him trying to save the man who had taught him how to fish and sail a boat—the man who had stood by Harry's side and shown him how to repair the house. They had been covered in mud together, and afterward, Arik had washed the boy's hands. He'd been patient, listening to her son's conversation and treating him with kindness. In truth, he been more of a father to Harry than William had ever been.

And in that same moment, she saw the barrel of the pistol pointing all too close to her son.

Juliana ran forward to pull him back, not caring about anything else except protecting him. "Harry, don't!"

Arik released the viscount and grabbed Harry, pushing him to the ground as the gun exploded. Her son struck the floor, and blood pooled upon the marble.

Juliana's scream of anguish ripped from her throat, her soul tearing apart as she dropped to her knees. Harry was unmoving, and his shirt was covered in blood. She couldn't hear the words she was saying, couldn't grasp the horror of what was happening.

Tears blinded her as she prayed with all her might. *Please be all right. Oh dear God, please let him live.* In that moment, nothing else mattered. Not the way William had treated her...not the shame she would suffer for his deception...not even the night she'd spent in Arik's arms. All that mattered was knowing her child would survive.

She gathered him into her arms, sobbing

uncontrollably. Harry's eyes were wide, and he struggled to breathe. "Mama," he murmured, before he closed his eyes. Terror filled her that her baby, the joy of her life, was dying and there was nothing she could do to save him.

The viscount stared at both of them, before he bolted toward the door, pushing his way past the servants who had come running at the sound of the gunshot. Juliana let him go, too worried about Harry to care about the man who had shot him. There was time to find William later. Her son was all that mattered now.

"Juliana," came Arik's voice.

She glanced up at him, and saw that he was on his knees beside her. His face held a gray pallor, and it was only then that she saw the raw flesh and the hole that had torn apart his chest. *Dear God, no.*

She stared with dawning realization. The blood all over Harry was not his own. It was Arik's, from when he'd tried to save the boy's life. Her son was moving in and out of consciousness, and it soon became clear that he'd struck his head on the marble floor when Arik had pushed him away.

"Fetch a doctor!" she called out to the servants. "Please, he needs help!"

Arik couldn't die. Not like this. Yet, there was an eerie stillness present, almost as if time had ceased. There was no bustle of activity, no sounds of anything at all. The room began to blur, as if she was losing consciousness. Juliana fought to remain alert, dimly aware that the Viking was holding her hand.

"Is Harry...all right?" he asked.

"Y-yes. He hit his head when you pushed him out of the way." Already her son was opening his eyes, crying as he rubbed the sore spot on his head. She couldn't stop her own tears, both relief that Harry was unharmed, but agony that Arik had been shot.

"A doctor is coming to help you," she insisted, though it was not true. Juliana untied his cravat and tried to stop the blood flow from his wound. "We'll fix this, I promise you. You—you won't die."

But he reached out to touch her cheek, wiping a tear away. "I do not belong in your world, and I never did. I was already dead when I came to you." He reached out to touch her face, but the caress was so light, she could barely feel it.

She was going to lose him. And the dawning realization turned her heart into ice. "Stay with me, Arik."

"The nights I spent with you were worth an eternity." When Juliana took his other hand, she saw that it was becoming transparent. "And I will never regret giving up the time I had left to save your son."

Arik lay down beside the boy, and Harry sat up, his expression sober. "I don't want you to die, Mr. Thorgrim. I want you to be my father."

He took the Viking's hand in his small one, and Arik tried to venture a smile. "When I pass from this life, I will remain with you," he swore. "Here." He touched the boy's heart and Harry stared back, his countenance stricken.

"Don't leave me," she pleaded. But already she could see that it was happening. Arik's presence grew more ghostly. Within moments, he would be gone. She was losing the man she had fallen in love with...but in return, he'd given her back Harry's life.

"I will always be with you," he said. "You will never forget me."

"You have to stay," Juliana told him, her voice breaking with the pain that devastated her. "If not for me, then for our child." She was searching for any means of binding him to her, of giving him a reason to hold on.

A faint smile creased his mouth. "Tell him about me, when he is grown." Arik stroked her hair, and she thought of Grelod's warning, that a child born from two moments in time could not live.

A thousand prayers came to her lips, but she couldn't voice a single one. Instead, all she could say was, "I love you."

Arik pressed his hand to her womb and murmured, "When one life ends, another begins."

And after the last breath left him, her Viking's body disappeared in her arms.

ChAPTER NINE

Juliana didn't know how long she wept, but her knees grew numb and her heart had turned to stone. When the footman returned, he appeared startled. "My lady, are you unwell?"

Juliana raised her tearstained eyes to his. Her emotions were bruised and raw, and she hardly knew what had happened anymore. Arik had died to save her son, and she felt as if someone had torn her life apart. It was then that she noticed Harry was gone. "Have you seen my son?"

"Harry is upstairs in the nursery," the man answered. "I saw him only a moment ago."

She didn't understand what he meant by that. How could her son be here one moment and upstairs the next?

"What about Lord Hawthorne? Where is he?" she managed to ask. The blackguard deserved to be arrested for what he'd done.

"Lord Hawthorne?" the footman appeared confused. "I have not seen him, my lady. Were you expecting him to pay a call upon you?"

Confusion muddled her mind at that. The man was acting as if nothing at all had happened. Hadn't William's gun gone off? Or did no one remember that he'd been here?

"Are you certain? He was just here a moment ago."

The footman shook his head slowly. "No, my lady. He was never here."

She stilled at that and looked around. There was no blood upon the floor, no fallen pistol. It was as if nothing at all had happened.

Her heart began pounding, and she didn't at all understand what had happened. It was as if a single moment in time had vanished. If William had never been here, then had he truly killed Arik Thorgrim?

The footman reached out a hand to help her up. "Are you certain you're all right, my lady? Did you fall, perhaps?"

In other words, he believed she was seeing and hearing things. Which was entirely possible, given that she'd just watched a Viking disappear before her eyes.

"I—I don't know." Juliana got to her feet and mumbled an excuse about going to see Harry. She ascended the stairs, turning over the events in her mind.

She didn't know what was real and what was not. It was as if Arik had disappeared without a trace, as if he'd never existed. And if that was true, then William could not have killed him.

When she reached her son's room, she found Harry playing with his tin soldiers. "Hello, Mama," he greeted her.

Hearing his voice brought a rush of thankfulness, and she hurried forward to embrace him. "Are you feeling all right, Harry?"

He nodded in answer to her question and continued to arrange the tin soldiers, making battle noises.

Juliana forced herself to sit down. "Did you...happen to see Mr. Thorgrim a little while ago?"

"No, I haven't seen him in weeks. When is he coming back?"

A rush of relief filled her. She hadn't wanted him to remember watching Arik die. If, in fact, he had. But at least Harry remembered him—that was something. She rested her palm against her stomach, praying that their unborn child was still alive.

"I don't know if he will come back," she said honestly. "But I hope he can."

Tears blinded her, and she turned away from her son, trying to control them. The past few days had awakened her from the shadowed life she'd lived. With Arik, she had found the strength to fight for what she wanted. No longer did she care about scandal or what others thought. She had fallen in love with a man who was bold, passionate, and fiercely loyal. He would not want her to lose her courage now. Not after the sacrifice he'd made.

"It will be all right, Harry," she told her son. "I will take care of us." She intended to speak with Lord Hawthorne and demand a settlement for them. After the deception he had pulled, he owed her compensation for the years he'd stolen. Then, too, she wanted to know whether he had played any part in the Viking's death.

Juliana started toward the door, and she suddenly spied Arik's blade resting upon a nearby desk. The sight of the dagger, back where it belonged, made her falter.

She had been certain her son had brought the knife down with him, planning to attack the viscount. Yet now, it was back in his room, untouched. She took the blade, feeling the wooden hilt against her hands. It was heavy, with runes carved upon it. When she gripped the weapon, she felt a connection, as if there was something she had to do.

The duke, she realized. The duke should know what had just happened.

The urge to leave was so strong, she excused herself from Harry and exited the room. The moment she did, she nearly collided with Grelod.

"Could you watch over Harry?" Juliana asked. "I need to speak with His Grace, the Duke of Somerford."

"Of course," her maid responded. The old woman's expression held sympathy, and it was enough to bring back the rise of tears she was fighting back. "My lady, I am sorry for all of this. I should never have invoked what wasn't meant to be. It was a prayer, that's all. One I never thought would be answered in this way."

Juliana nodded. "I don't regret any of what happened between us. Arik Thorgrim was a gift I never expected. I only wish there was a way to bring him back."

Her maid shook her head with sadness. "Such magic is far beyond me." She moved forward to take Juliana's hand. "I believe in many things, my lady. Fate. Magic. Second chances." She squeezed her palm. "But he was never meant to dwell in this time."

Juliana knew that. And yet, she couldn't quite let go of hope. Prayers had brought Arik Thorgrim across time to love her. Her hand moved down to her womb, and she prayed that there was a reason to keep him here.

One strong enough to pull a man from eternity.

Juliana waited for hours at the duke's town house before he returned, just after sunset. She rose when he entered the parlor, and a moment later, he closed the door behind him.

"What has happened? Is it my son?"

She unwrapped the blade and held it out to him. "Arik disappeared in my arms. One moment he was there, and the next..." Fresh grief washed over her, as she told him of the gun firing, of Arik dying, and of his disappearance. As strange as it all sounded, she felt the need to confess everything to the duke.

"I know that he's gone," Juliana finished. "But I can't quite let go of him."

Arik had spoken of the moment of his death, a thousand years ago...and of how he'd been caught between worlds. She knew it was impossible for a man to die twice, and a part of her desperately wanted to believe that he could somehow still be near.

The duke crossed the space and took the knife from her. "You said he died to save your son?"

She bit her lip hard. "Yes. He pushed Harry away and the bullet took him instead." A tear escaped her and she admitted, "He spent his last days trying to help Harry and me." A bitter smile crossed her face. "He said it was his way of earning a place in the afterworld. I suppose he's done that now."

Duke Somerford held the blade in his hands, testing the weight. It was as if he hadn't heard a word she'd spoken. "You need not worry about providing for your son. I will help both of you."

She sank into a chair. "I don't care about that anymore. I would give up every last farthing if I could have Arik back. I just...can't believe he's dead." She couldn't stop her tears, and her fists dug into her skirts. It hurt so much to know that she would never see his handsome face again or feel his arms around her.

The duke said nothing, but let her weep. In his hands, he turned over the ancient knife. "My son and I fought with bitter words on the night he left. I never saw him again. But somehow, a part of him returned to me in Arik Thorgrim. He had…some of my Eric's memories. I have no way to explain it."

When she studied him, he seemed far older in that moment. It was as if time had ravaged his face, leaving him to grieve. "I knew he wasn't my son," the duke continued, "but in the days I spent with him, I felt as if I had Eric back with me."

"Arik was not of this world," Juliana confessed. "He was a Viking. Somehow he crossed through time to be here…and I think your son crossed back."

It sounded like madness to say such a thing, but the duke appeared to accept it far too easily.

"He told me that," the older man agreed, "and he knew things that only Eric knew." He rested his hands against the back of a chair and met her gaze with grief that mirrored her own. "I don't think either of them will ever return."

Juliana crossed the room and took his hand. "A part of his spirit does live on."

She touched her stomach lightly and it took a moment before understanding dawned in his eyes. There was a faint gleam of hope that transcended the sadness between them. "Bring your son back to Somerford. I will give both of you a home with me, if you wish to stay there."

His generous offer was something she'd never expected. "I would be grateful." She moved to stand beside him. Outside the parlor window, she saw the full moon casting its beams over the house.

"If I could bring him back for you, I would," the duke said quietly.

But both of them knew it was impossible.

Arik drifted upon the sea for endless hours, leaning back within his longship. The sky was gray, like Juliana's eyes. And though he believed he was sailing on to Asgard, that this was truly the end, he could not stop thinking of her.

She haunted him in a way he'd never expected. Her quiet smile, and the way she'd stood up to William, showed a courage that he admired.

By the gods, he'd been so wrong. Asgard was not the afterlife he sought. He cared nothing for the glory of battle or bringing honor to his ancestors. An eternity of happiness lay in Juliana's arms, not in a kingdom of Viking warriors.

But that choice was no longer his.

The mists encircled him, and in the distance, he saw the faint glimmer of lights. The echo of voices crossed the sea, and he saw the face of a goddess rising from the mists. He did not doubt it was Freya.

Do you seek to join us here?

He could not answer that. What he wanted was to remain at Juliana's side, to watch her body grow round with his child. To hear his son's newborn cry and raise Harry as another son.

I want to stay with Juliana, he answered honestly.

Such is not possible. Your body perished in battle and your soul must join ours. You asked for more time, and that was given to you. Now, you must join your brothers in Valhalla.

The answer was exactly as he'd expected. But then, the gods were known to weave mortals' lives in unexpected patterns. If they had granted him time once before, they could do it again.

I would give up my eternity for a lifetime with her.

The voices of his ancestors seemed to fade away, the lights growing dimmer. He might have angered the gods by rejecting his chance at immortality, but it was the truth.

The love of a woman is not a reason to turn your back upon immortality. The goddess's voice held unveiled fury, and he waited for an invisible blow to strike him down. Freya was not known for mercy.

I am bound to her in the life of our unborn child. Even this afterworld cannot part us, he told her.

She will lose the child. Then there will be nothing binding you to the mortal world.

From within the boat, he felt the sea begin to stir. The waters grew rough, and he grasped the mast as the winds heightened. It was a physical manifestation of Freya's wrath, and he fought to hold his footing. The storm grew violent, lightning flashing from Odin above. Thunder rumbled, and water crashed against the side of the boat.

Yet he felt no fear. He was already dead, and he'd lost everything worth fighting for. From deep inside came the need to lash back at the storm. He stood against the wind and the biting rain, his fury rising. The wind battered at him, but he released a roar of frustration and grief.

Not yet, he told the goddess, casting back the same words she had told him on the night he'd died. *You cannot have my soul yet. It belongs to her.*

But he heard only malicious laughter in response. *A life must be given to take your place.*

He sank to his knees in the boat, his head bowed. Grief roared through him, for he would never regret giving up his life for Harry's. Nor would he want Juliana to lose their unborn child.

He understood now that being a father meant more

than offering protection and shelter. A child took away pieces of a man's heart. Even in the afterworld, he would carry the memory of the young boy smiling up at him as they smeared mud into Juliana's house.

Now he realized the agony he'd forced his father to endure when he'd left Rogaland, never to return. With each year Arik had been gone, Valdr Thorgrim had suffered.

Regret swelled within him, as he realized this was his punishment. He would not live to grow old with Juliana or watch their children grow to manhood.

But he would wait for her in Asgard. No matter how many centuries it took.

TWO WEEKS LATER

The journey back to the Duke of Somerford's estate was arduous, and Juliana wanted to weep during every last mile. She was no stranger to heartache, but the letter in her hand was a tangible reminder of all that had been lost.

Grelod had remained silent during the journey, not answering any questions, but simply keeping to herself. Harry had slept in Juliana's lap, and she'd taken comfort that her boy would now live in a place that he could call home.

In his letter, the duke had given orders for Juliana to live upon the estate and make it hers until his son returned. She was grateful to have a place of her own, even if it meant remaining away from London. Here,

Harry could grow into manhood without others ridiculing him for her mistakes.

And as for William, the duke had written that his solicitor would ensure that Lord Hawthorne would face censure for the way he'd deceived her with a false marriage. Although it seemed that all of the events surrounding the shooting had been erased, she had to trust that somehow justice would be served.

The coach drew to a stop, and Juliana woke Harry. "We're here at our new home, darling."

Harry yawned and stretched, before he bounded out the door to hold it open for them. Their dog, Bartholomew, jumped down, his tail wagging. Juliana smiled and let the footman help her out, ruffling her son's hair. She clutched the duke's letter and walked along the gravel pathway toward the house.

The country estate was larger than Hawthorne House, with a brick front and tall windows. Ivy edged the far wall, and she caught a glimpse of pink roses in the gardens. It was the sort of home she'd dreamed of once. And for now, she would try to live each day as if it were her last.

Juliana was about to give the footman instructions about their belongings, when suddenly she glimpsed a tall figure crossing the grounds. He wore a bottle-green coat and his hair was longer than was fashionable.

Was he real?

Her heart started beating so fast, she couldn't breathe anymore. Seizing the hem of her skirts, she broke into a full run. The man turned, and she saw Arik Thorgrim, in the flesh. Despite all that had happened, he was here.

Juliana could hardly see the man through her tears, and when she reached him, she threw herself into his arms. "You're alive." The two words couldn't possible convey her joy, and she embraced him tightly. Though she didn't know how any of this was possible when she had watched him die in her arms, she didn't ask. None of it mattered, and she buried her face in his chest, holding him close.

But he wasn't holding her in return. Instead, he gently extricated her arms from his neck. "Do I know you?"

His voice held a slight accent, as if English was not his native language. She studied him, noting the dark eyes and the longer hair. Outwardly, it appeared that the man she loved was standing right here. And yet, he didn't seem to remember her.

Her heart utterly sank. What if this was not Arik Thorgrim, returned from his voyage at sea?

What if it was Eric Fielding, the Marquess of Thorgraham?

CHAPTER TEN

The young woman staring back at him looked about ready to weep. He didn't know what to say to her, but the moment she'd thrown herself into his arms, it had been like a jolt of lightning.

She was familiar to him somehow, though he couldn't understand in what way. The soft scent of her skin, the honeyed hair, reminded him of a fey spirit.

"I—I'm so sorry. I thought you were...someone I once..." She shook her head, unable to speak. "I should not have thrown myself at you like that."

He wanted to ease this beautiful woman's embarrassment, for he didn't mind at all that she'd embraced him. She clearly held strong feelings for him, and from deep within came the desire to know the truth. Who was she? And how had he known her?

Other memories began surfacing. He knew the taste of this woman's lips, and he sensed the softness of her body.

"There was more between us, wasn't there?" he said. Without asking permission, he took her arm in his. He wanted to speak with her alone, to understand what had happened between them. But he was interrupted by a small boy who came running forward, trailed by a dog. "Mr. Thorgrim! I've missed you!"

The child threw himself forward, gripping his leg. It was a shock to suddenly be hugged by a young boy for no apparent reason. The dog's tail was wagging, and the animal jumped up, licking him with enthusiasm.

Gently, he pushed the dog down and ruffled the boy's hair. "I am glad to see you, too, boy." He struggled to remember the child's name, but could not do so.

"You promised to teach me how to hunt," the boy said. "Can we go tomorrow? I'm going to live here now."

The boy's eyes held such hope, he nodded. "I will teach you." Joy brightened the boy's expression, and he hugged him again.

Warmth filled him at the child's affection, easing his immense loneliness. "Over in the gardens, there is a large tree with a ladder and a small shelter," he told the boy. "You could go exploring." He pointed toward the gate, and as soon as he'd made the offer, the child was off and running toward it with the dog following.

The young woman watched her son, a sudden softness stealing over her face. Her name was on the edge of his memory, taunting him. He led her inside the house, wanting to know more about her.

"Your father sent me with a letter," she told him. "He...gave me permission to stay here." Her face dimmed a moment and she said, "I suppose you know that he died a few weeks ago, the night you—that is, the last time I saw you."

Another memory slammed into him without warning. *A life must be given to take your place.*

His head ached as he tried to understand what had happened. It was as if the memories were scattered pieces of a larger vision, but he had not yet put them together.

For the past two weeks, he'd felt restless…as if his life had been violently disrupted. The servants had welcomed him back, treating him as though he'd been lost at sea. His memories had been tangled up, for this did not seem to be his life or his house.

And yet it was. He'd walked through each of the rooms, and faint memories were evoked in this place. He knew the portraits and the names of the servants.

But it felt as if he had been put back in a place where he did not belong. He could not reconcile himself to this house or this life…until now. Until he had seen this beautiful woman.

She removed her bonnet, and he glimpsed hair the color of dark gold. Clear gray eyes studied him, and she seemed to have gathered her composure. But still, she appeared despondent that he didn't remember her.

He led her into the drawing room and rang for tea. And the moment they were alone, he crossed toward her and sat beside her. "You *are* familiar to me, though I cannot remember your name."

Her smile was halfhearted. "I don't think you remember anything." She swallowed hard. "You aren't the person I thought you were."

He didn't know what she meant by that, but it bothered him. "And who am I supposed to be?"

"You'd think me mad if I told you the truth." She shook her head, refusing to say any more.

A harsh emotion rose up within him, and his frustration intensified. He didn't like seeing her unhappy, especially when he was the cause of it. What was he supposed to remember?

"Close your eyes," he commanded. "Tell me about the man you sought."

She obeyed and said, "He was strong and bold. A little dangerous, even."

When she spoke, her words seemed to unlock memories. He saw himself kissing her, while her body was bathed in moonlight. Within him, there came the need to conquer, to provoke her desire.

"He wanted to protect me and my son," she murmured. "And this belonged to him."

From her cloak she withdrew a knife. When he examined it, he saw an ancient weapon that fit his hand as if it was made for it.

This was mine, given to me by my father. Not the duke, but instead by the man who had taught him how to hunt and how to fight.

There was a softness in her expression, of a woman who had loved deeply. Her dark blond hair framed a face that haunted him. More memories flooded through him, of walking along the coast with her, watching her son run through the sand. There was a sense of rightness being with her.

He reached out to touch her chin, drawing her closer. Her eyes welled up with emotion, but she did not turn him away. The instinct to claim her soft mouth was too strong, and he leaned in for a kiss. The moment their lips touched, physical memories came crashing upon him. He didn't know where they had come from, but he *did* remember this woman. He remembered joining with her on board a ship, the waves rocking the vessel. He remembered touching her, watching her come apart as she arched and cried out his name.

He remembered surrendering his life to save her son.

"Arik," she whispered.

The name was slightly different, and yet, it was right. He continued kissing her, and when her hands moved to his hair, he pulled her in so close, it felt as if their bodies were merged.

"Juliana," he breathed against her mouth. "I do remember you." The visions were fragmented, but his emotions broke through the fog of memory.

She gave a tremulous smile, and he could see her fighting back tears. He kissed her again, feeling the rise of longing within him. Her arms wrapped around him, and she met his mouth with desire of her own. Past and present collided, and he was powerless to resist the roaring needs.

He gazed at her, feeling the wildness coursing in his blood. Right now, he wanted her desperately, as if a barbaric part of him had risen to the forefront.

"We were together not long ago," he reminded her. The vivid image of her naked body was branded in his mind, and the way he'd taken her hard. "I remember touching you. Claiming you."

He cupped her face, and she rested her palms upon his chest. There was uncertainty in her eyes, but her cheeks held the flush of her own desire. "You did, yes."

"And there was a child." He drew his hand down to her flat stomach, wondering if he had only dreamed of this.

"There could be," she murmured. "I believe it is true." She reached up to touch his hair, skimming her fingers down his face. "Do you remember how it was between us?"

He pressed her back, kissing her hard, until both of them were breathless. "What do you think, *kjære*?"

"When you behave like this, I know it's you," she whispered. "My Viking, returned to me."

And so he was. The tangled memories seemed to grow clearer, and he understood that Freya had indeed granted his wish to return, and he had been placed within this life.

Arik lifted Juliana up, and she had no choice but to hold tight for balance. The scent of her skin pulled him in, and he kissed her throat. "I gave up my eternity for you. And I would do it again without question."

Juliana stared into his eyes and could not deny the truth before her. The man she loved was here again, and the joy inside was so great, she felt as if she could soar upon it.

It saddened her that the duke was now gone. And yet…she wondered if he might have been the reason Arik had returned. Somerford's death had been unexpected, but perhaps when the old man had died, he had found a way to plead for mercy in the afterlife. She rested her cheek against Arik's shoulder, so grateful that he was alive.

The man who stood before her now was not the duke's son as she'd feared…he was indeed Arik Thorgrim, the man she loved. The intensity in his eyes pulled her under, and she understood his dark need to claim her. Right now she wanted to join with him, to be one with this man.

"I don't know how you were brought back to me," she said softly. "But I love you, and I intend to savor each moment we have together."

He held her as if she weighed nothing, and though he was fully clothed, she could feel the hard ridge of his desire nestled against her.

"I was given the chance to join my family in Valhalla," he admitted against her mouth. "But it was no longer what I wanted. I could not go back when my spirit was bound to yours."

She rested her cheek against his, reveling in the

hardness of his body against her own. "And my heart is bound to you."

He drew back and narrowed his gaze at her. "You're going to be my wife, Juliana. No man will ever lay claim to you, save me."

It wasn't a question, but she already knew her answer. "I will, yes. Though it will likely scandalize all of London."

"I don't care about them. Only you," he said. "I love you, *kjære.* And you are mine."

She smiled at him. "I never imagined that I would spend the rest of my life with a man who brings a battle-ax into the ballroom."

"And I will bring it again if any man dares to threaten you."

She laughed, leaning in to kiss him once more. For a time, he remained where he was, holding her close. "Once, I believed I had to die before I would ever find such happiness." He kissed her softly. "But I've found it in you."

EPILOGUE

JUNE, 1812

Arik walked alongside his wife while Harry ran along the shoreline with the dog Bartholomew. Juliana carried their infant son Gregory, who was gurgling and beaming. Never in his life had he imagined that he would have such a family—a wife who stole his breath every time he looked at her, and two sons who gave him such pride.

"You cannot imagine how many letters I've received from Grandmama," Juliana was saying. "Apparently our secret wedding last year was the talk of the ton. The gossips are all wanting to know how a fisherman's daughter caught a duke for a husband."

He shrugged. "Perhaps they should be asking how a Viking won the heart of a goddess."

Juliana's soft smile was filled with love. "It must be the way you fought for her."

He took her hand in his and added, "William Arthur was a fool to let you go. And I hope he loses every last penny he owns."

This past spring, Arik had taken his seat in the House of Lords, watching the proceedings. It was not unlike a Viking *thing,* where his father and other advisors had made decisions regarding laws and had passed judgment. Though he had spoken rarely while Parliament was in session, he was starting to gain a sense of his new position as the Duke of Somerford. He had the older man's notes and ledgers to assist him as well. And as time went on, the memories given to him by Eric Fielding, the duke's son, had gradually begun to fade away.

The most gratifying part of his new life as the duke was witnessing the humiliation of William Arthur, the Viscount Hawthorne. The viscount had lost a great deal of his fortune, gambling at White's. Two of Arik's friends, Jack Warwick and Lord Gabriel Stanhope, had assisted him in bringing Hawthorne into greater ruin by appealing to the man's greed.

Strangely, Hawthorne had no memory of visiting Juliana on the morning he'd demanded a share of the Viking hoard. It was as if the shooting had never happened. Neither he, nor Juliana, could understand it. It was as if time had reversed itself, erasing the deed entirely. No one remembered anything surrounding his death.

Perhaps Freya had smoothed out the edges of time, granting him Juliana as the reward for his sacrifice. Or perhaps the old duke had taken his place in the afterworld when the goddess had claimed, *a life must be given to take your place.* There was no way to be certain. But Arik believed that the strongest reason for his staying was their son, Gregory, who held him bound to the woman he loved.

Harry was running along the sand, picking up shells

and other treasures, when suddenly he called out to them, "Mama! Papa! Come and see what I've found!"

Arik closed the distance, striding along the beach until he reached his adopted son. He knelt down on the sand, wondering what sort of shell Harry had found.

Instead, Harry picked up a gold ring. "I've found Viking gold, don't you see? It must be part of a treasure!"

Arik studied the ring Harry had found, while the boy continued to dig in the wet sand with a large stick. A jolt caught him as he recognized it as one his father, Valdr, had given to him, long ago. He slid it onto his finger, and he glanced up at the sky, wondering if his father could see them now. He wanted to believe that there was peace between them and forgiveness.

Juliana kissed him lightly, then turned back toward Harry. "You do realize that he's going to keep searching for more treasures, now that he's found gold."

"Do you desire more gold, my wife?" Arik asked, teasing her. "Shall I go a-viking to bring it back for you?"

"I don't need any treasures at all," Juliana answered. "I have everything I ever dreamed of, right here."

If you enjoyed *A Viking for the Viscountess,* look for its sequel, *A Maiden for the Marquess,* coming in 2015. Also, reviews are always appreciated if you want to let others know what you thought of the book.

Would you like me to e-mail you when I have a new book out? You may sign up for my newsletter at www.michellewillingham.com. I only send e-mails when I have a new release, and you may unsubscribe at any time. Your e-mail address will never be shared with third parties or sold.

A Viking for the Viscountess is part of the mini-series, *A Most Peculiar Season.* Arik and Juliana make special appearances in other books, beginning with *Scandal on His Doorstep,* by Deborah Hale (available in December of 2014).

A baby is left on Jack Warwick's doorstep. And the notorious rake doesn't know if the child is his.

Jack shares a Mayfair town house with two friends, and a note left with the baby suggests one of the three bachelors is the father...but which one? And who will care for the child until they can locate her mother?

Jack can think of only one woman he would trust with such a delicate task. Annabelle Robb, the penniless widow of his cousin, has been too proud to accept his financial support. Enlisting her help with the baby is the perfect excuse to provide for the woman who was once his dearest friend.

Annabelle agrees, with great reluctance. She cannot turn her back on an abandoned child, for both she and Jack know the pain of being unwanted. Yet she's afraid of spending more time with the man who broke her heart so long ago, when he never even knew of her infatuation.

Jack doesn't know if he is the baby's father, but he vows to reform his ways. Yet the more time he spends with Annabelle, the more he is torn between a sense of duty to find and marry the child's mother...and his growing desire for Annabelle!

Visit www.deborahhale.com for more details.

Would you like to know whether Margaret Andrews ever found a husband with all of his teeth? Enjoy a free sample of *Unlaced by the Outlaw* by Michelle Willingham, available December 2, 2014.

Excerpt from

UNLACED BY THE OUTLAW
by Michelle Willingham

CHAPTER ONE

LONDON, 1815

Her sister was missing.

Most older sisters would leave such a terrible problem in the hands of their parents. Or possibly alert the authorities. Margaret Andrews did neither.

For one, she knew exactly who had kidnapped Amelia. Second, she knew that the blackguard intended to force her sister to wed him. And third, Margaret had suffered untold humiliation when that same awful man had abandoned her only days before their wedding three years ago. Lord Lisford might have shattered her girlish dreams, humiliating her in the face of society, but Margaret would never let the same thing happen to her baby sister. This was more than a dangerous situation—this was her opportunity for vengeance.

It didn't matter that it was the middle of the night or that she was the daughter of a baron. The man who had wronged her was about to destroy Amelia's life, and Margaret was *not* about to stand aside and let it happen. She'd beg the devil himself, if she thought he could help her.

Cain Sinclair was the next best thing.

A flutter of nerves caught her stomach as her coach pulled to a stop in front of the inn where he was staying. It was nearly midnight, and she'd left Lady Rumford's ball the moment she'd learned of Amelia's disappearance. Margaret was still wearing the sage-green silk gown with white gloves, for she'd not taken the time to change.

This was a very bad idea. What was she thinking, venturing into a public inn while wearing a ball gown?

But it couldn't be helped. *Please let him be there,* she prayed. The Highlander was a man she'd known for nine years. From the moment she'd laid eyes on him, she'd sensed that he was the sort of man her mother had warned her about.

Taller than most men, he had broad shoulders and lean muscles. His piercing blue eyes and black hair gave him the look of a fallen angel. He wasn't a gentleman and he didn't care what anyone thought of him.

Ruthless was the best word to describe him. And when he wanted something, he never stopped until he got it.

Unfortunately, what he wanted was *her.*

She took a deep breath and stepped out of the coach. Her footman eyed the inn and shook his head. "Miss Andrews, I think you should wait inside the coach. I'll go and find Mr. Sinclair on your behalf."

That was the sensible thing to do. It was what her mother would want. But she knew, without a single doubt, that Sinclair would ignore the footman and do whatever he wanted to. Whereas if she pleaded with him, there was a chance he might help her.

With every moment she sat in this coach, Lord Lisford was taking her sister farther north, toward Scotland. Time was critical, and what did she care if it was not an establishment a lady would dare to enter? She was already ruined. After five Seasons, Margaret knew what the ton thought of her. They believed she was to blame for Lord Lisford abandoning her on her wedding day.

The familiar ache of bitterness stiffened her spine. It was high time the viscount paid the price for what he'd done to her. And if he thought he could hurt her sister without serious consequences, he was sadly mistaken.

Margaret ignored her servant and marched straight toward the door. For a moment, she paused with her hand upon the doorknob. *Go back,* her conscience ordered. But instead, she gathered her courage and opened the door.

The haze of tobacco cloaked the room, while the scent of ale filled the space. Men were playing cards in one corner, while others busied themselves with getting drunk as soon as possible.

She stared at each of the men until at last she located Sinclair. He didn't move, but his mouth tightened when she stepped closer. Her presence was as out of place as a pig in a ballroom, and every male eye fastened upon her.

Her conscience was still screeching at the idea. *Get out of here! Ladies do not associate with men at an inn. You cannot be here.*

Cain Sinclair's icy blue eyes regarded her as if she'd lost her mind. And perhaps she had, since she'd gone to such lengths to seek his help.

"You don't belong here, lass," he said.

"Amelia's been taken by Lord Lisford. You have to help me find her." Margaret crossed her arms, staring coolly at a drunkard whose attention was fixed upon her bosom.

How did you think these men would react to your presence? her common sense chided. *They're nothing but rogues and vagrants. Any one of them would attack you, and then where would you be?*

The Highlander leaned back in his chair, his long black hair falling past his shoulders. He wore a brown-and-green tartan, and his white shirtsleeves were rolled against his forearms. A faint scar edged his lower arm, a reminder that he'd been in many fights. Somehow, it made her feel somewhat safer, knowing that Sinclair could protect her far better than the elderly footman who had accompanied her.

"Come with me, and I'll tell you more about what happened," Margaret urged. The sooner she left this place, the better she would feel. The question was whether or not he would help her.

"Do your parents know?" he asked softly.

She shrugged. "I didn't tell them. I want to find Amelia before any harm is done."

They would find out soon enough. But more than that, she felt a sense of responsibility. *She* was supposed to have chaperoned Amelia at the ball. If she'd remained at her sister's side at every moment, this wouldn't have happened.

Her guilt was a hair shirt against her conscience. This was her fault, without question. And she had to atone for it, no matter the cost to her own reputation.

Sinclair took a slow drink of his ale, studying her. She couldn't guess what he was thinking, but he needed to hurry up.

"Why did you come to me, lass, instead of the police?" His lazy tone held a hint of wickedness, and she faltered.

"Because I—"

Because I know you'll find her. I know you won't let any harm come to her, and I trust you more than any man.

She drew closer and reached for his hand. It felt as if she'd thrown out every shred of decent behavior. A wildness thrummed in her blood as her fingers laced in his.

"Because I need your help," she whispered.

His thumb brushed the edge of her palm in a silent caress that echoed deep inside. His rough hands were callused, but his touch was light enough to set her senses on fire. What did that say about her, that she would be so attracted to a man so inappropriate?

She was a good girl. She obeyed the rules, listened to her parents, and never wore a gown with a daring neckline. All her life, she'd been a model of proper behavior.

And yet, right now, she realized that she was asking this man to come with her. To be alone with her in a coach for hours on end.

Don't do this, her sense of propriety begged. *You cannot behave in this way. It's not right.*

But she met his gaze steadily and said, "Please."

Enjoyed the sample? Read the rest by ordering
Unlaced by the Outlaw at
www.michellewillingham.com/book/unlaced-outlaw/.
It is available in print, e-book, and audio. Although it is book
four in the Secrets in Silk series, the books can be read in
any order. If you'd like to begin with book one, *Undone by
the Duke*, here's another excerpt for you to try.

UNDONE BY THE DUKE
by Michelle Willingham

PROLOGUE

BALLALOCH, SCOTLAND
DECEMBER 1810

Jonathan Nottoway, the fourth Duke of Worthingstone, was staring down the barrel of a gun.

He supposed he ought to be feeling fear or even a sense of impending doom. Instead, Fate had a way of mocking him. His attacker wasn't a seasoned killer or a disgruntled tenant. No, he had the damnably bad luck to be threatened by a boy who wasn't even old enough to shave.

"Put the weapon down," he ordered. "You don't want to shoot me."

"Yes, I do." Anguish lined the boy's face, along with a single-minded purpose. "It's your fault. All of it."

The boy's hands started shaking, and Jonathan tried to take a step back. The gun would go off if his finger tightened even a fraction.

"And what, precisely, am I accused of?" He spoke softly, as if soothing a wounded animal. Glancing around, he saw none of his servants nearby. Not his groom or even a blessed footman. He supposed it was his own fault for snarling at them this morning to leave him the hell alone. They'd done just that.

The outside temperature was growing colder, and a few fat snowflakes fluttered from the sky. Jonathan had tethered his horse back near the frozen stream, so he didn't even have the option of riding away.

"You know what you've done," the boy spat. "Burned our homes and murdered the others."

Though Jonathan was aware of the Highland evictions, with landowners forcing the Scots out of their homes, he'd had nothing to do with that. His reasons for being in Scotland were purely financial. After purchasing this land a year ago, he'd come to inspect the crumbling house that went with it.

Now it was perfectly clear why land stewards were meant to handle such details.

"I'm not the one who set your home on fire," Jonathan said. "And I've killed no one."

"Your men did," the boy insisted. He raised the gun to Jonathan's chest. "When you're dead, the burnings will stop."

"I'm not certain who you think I am," he said to the boy, "but I can assure you, you have the wrong man."

"You're the Earl of Strathland," the boy said, his eyes brimming up with tears. "And because of you, my mother was burned."

"I am not the earl," Jonathan began. "You've made a mistake. I only came to—"

His words broke off when the gun fired.

CHAPTER ONE

Victoria Andrews knelt at her sister's feet, her mouth full of pins. With a careful eye, she judged that the hem was exactly the right length.

"Is it finished yet?" Amelia complained. "I've been standing here for years."

Victoria pulled another pin from her mouth, ignoring her sister's theatrics. "Hold still. Just a few more stitches."

The morning gown had belonged to their sister Margaret once, but with the help of some new fabric, Victoria had completely remade the skirt and bodice. She'd stitched delicate strips of blue silk to yards of white muslin, so as to give the illusion of a striped fabric. The fitted waist emphasized the girlish lines of Amelia's figure in the latest style.

"Should we lower the neckline?" Amelia suggested. "It seems a bit prim."

"It's a day dress, not an evening gown." The curved neckline exposed a good portion of Amelia's throat, and the long sleeves with vandyked cuffs provided an air of modesty. As a last touch, Victoria had made pink roses from a tired pair of satin gloves and fastened the flowers to the waist.

Her sister preened in front of the dressing mirror, scooping her brown curls into a more formal arrangement on her head. "Toria, it's wonderful. I can't believe how lovely it is." With a delighted smile, Amelia threw her arms around her.

Victoria basked in the warm hug. "Happy Birthday."

"I'll wear it when I pay calls with Mother." Amelia brimmed with excitement, twirling around. Her sister was more than eager to leave Scotland for London, even if it was only to visit Aunt Charlotte for Christmas.

"And perhaps when I arrive, I'll become best friends with the sister of a handsome earl or…even a duke! He might see me at a distance…and fall in love."

Her voice grew hushed, and Victoria hid her amusement at Amelia's dramatics. "You're sixteen and not old enough to marry."

"Oh, I know *that.*" Amelia shrugged. "But he can pine for a few years." Her face brightened with a sudden thought. "You might find a husband, too."

When Victoria didn't respond, her sister's face fell. "You *are* coming to London, aren't you?" To Amelia, the idea of remaining secluded at home was like cutting off all her hair—unthinkable.

Truthfully, Victoria was perfectly content to remain within these four walls. Although they had lived in England for most of her life, the last five years had been spent in the western Highlands. Scotland had become her new home, although every time she looked out the window, the gnarled mountains reminded her of how stark and isolated this land was. In the distance, the snowcapped peak of Ben Nevis towered over the hills like a benevolent grandfather.

"I can't go with you," she told Amelia. "But you'll give Aunt Charlotte my best, won't you?"

"Toria." Amelia held on to her, not bothering to hide her dismay. "You can't stay inside this house forever. It's not right."

"You needn't worry about me." She smoothed an invisible wrinkle on Amelia's gown. "Mrs. Larson and Mr. MacKinloch will keep me company while you're away."

Her sister stepped back to look at her, a worried expression on her face. "Don't you...want to find a husband?" she asked softly. "Or have children one day?"

Victoria said nothing. The unbidden tears heated her eyelids, and she stared down at the floor. Of course she wanted that. She wanted a normal life, more than anything. But after so many years of living with fear, the possibility had stretched into an unreachable dream.

"You never leave this house," Amelia continued, "and I don't know what you're afraid of."

"I can't explain it. But it's impossible for me." Each time she drew close to the front door, her insides twisted into knots. She couldn't stop shaking, and the air choked off in her lungs, until she couldn't breathe.

"I wish I could go," Victoria whispered. "But it's better if you travel without me." She couldn't stop the physical overreaction, no matter how many times she'd tried to walk out into the garden.

Their hundred-year-old house had cozy rooms and polished oak floors that creaked. Made of stone, it sat atop a small hillside, overlooking fields of gorse and heather. The road leading from the house curved down toward rows of makeshift tents erected by the Highland refugees. Dozens of men and women had been evicted a few weeks ago, and her mother had allowed them to take shelter here. Victoria often watched the people, wondering about how they lived and whether or not they were all right. But not once had she spoken with them. Though she loved her home, it was also her prison.

For she hadn't gone outside in five years.

Victoria helped her sister out of the gown, and Amelia pleaded, "Will you unlace me, just a little? It itches dreadfully."

Her sister's stays were drawn tight, and the chemise was made of a rough buckram that wasn't entirely pleasant against the skin. Victoria loosened the laces, all the while studying the construction of the corset. It was functional, with no embroidery, and made from little more than whalebone, coarse fabric, and a steel busk.

Amelia sighed with relief as she scratched her skin. "I've heard there are women in London who don't wear stays at all. Can you imagine?"

"No, I can't." Though her own figure was slender enough that she could wear short stays instead of the longer ones, the idea of wearing only a draped gown with nothing beneath the bodice was scandalizing. "Our mother would never allow it."

"No, but I would happily burn this torturous garment, if I could."

Victoria hid her smile. "It's not so bad, really, when you're used to it." Yet, as she laced the corset again, a strange thought occurred to her. *I wonder if I could make something like this. Only something softer, more comfortable to wear.*

If the chemise were created out of a delicate material like satin or velvet, the fabric would cling to a woman's skin. Even the corset itself could be lined with silk.

Her hands stilled upon Amelia's back, the idea evolving and taking shape. Already she'd seen patterns for embroidered petticoats, made of fine lawn or muslin. Yet, she'd never seen a corset made out of anything except unyielding, coarse material. All of them were white, as if proclaiming a woman's purity.

Slowly, Victoria began to pull the laces tight, unable to stop turning the idea over in her mind. Was it possible to construct a corset out of silk or satin, or would it tear under pressure? Perhaps it could be made of buckram but covered in silk, with a double lining next to the skin.

The idea intrigued her with a challenge she'd never before attempted. She had no idea how long it would take to make such a complicated garment...and yet, she found herself wanting to try it.

There was an older set of stays she could take apart to study for a pattern, and she knew there were gowns belonging to her grandmother in the bottom of a trunk. If she took one of them apart tonight, she could—

"Victoria?" her sister prompted. "Aren't you going to help me get dressed again?"

"Of course. I'm sorry." She lifted her sister's woolen dress over the undergarment, but her mind was still caught up in the vision.

As Victoria buttoned her sister up, Amelia wouldn't let go of their argument. "Toria, you can't stay in Scotland. It's too dangerous for a woman alone. We heard gunshots yesterday when we were visiting the crofters."

"They're fighting again?"

Amelia nodded. "There's not enough space and barely enough food to feed them all. Some have talked of taking back the land and killing the Earl of Strathland."

Victoria moved to the window. In the distance, she could see the smoke curling from their camp fires. A child wandered outside in the snow, her hair covered with a plaid, her clothing hardly more than rags. It bothered her to see them suffering in this way. She wished her family had more to give away, but there were simply too many of the crofters. Worse, with the food shortages, it wasn't surprising that some would turn to stealing from each other, if it meant feeding their children. The winter was always difficult, and Victoria's mother had sent for more supplies from London, simply for their own survival.

"You can't stay here alone. Not while we're gone." Amelia's face tightened. "What if they attack the house?"

"We've given them sanctuary," Victoria reminded her. "There's no reason for them to turn against us. And it's only temporary until they find a new place to live." She wanted to believe that, praying that the MacKinlochs would leave before the fighting worsened.

"It isn't safe," her sister argued. "Without Father here..." Her words broke off, her eyes filling up with tears. Their father, Colonel Henry Andrews, now Baron Lanfordshire, had been fighting in Spain for the past three years. There was no way of knowing when he would return.

Or *if* he would return.

Victoria took her sister's hand in reassurance. "Most of the crofters don't even know I'm here. And the ones who do, know that I never leave the house. I'm no threat to anyone."

Her sister fell silent, and she took it to mean Amelia had finally given up. Good. There was no sense in entertaining ideas that would never happen. Victoria took the white and blue gown and picked up her thimble, intending to start sewing the hem.

Instead, Amelia walked over and took the gown from her hands. "I want to see this gown on you."

"Amelia, no. Really, I—"

"We're nearly the same size. Let's see what it looks like." Before she could protest, her sister started unbuttoning the gray merino gown Victoria was wearing. With great reluctance, she forced herself to stand still while Amelia helped her into the muslin dress. "Careful, or you'll tear the sleeves."

She stood before the mirror while Amelia fastened the four buttons lining the back of the gown and tied the sash. Although the waistline fit well enough, her bust was too small, and the bodice gaped slightly. She needed an extra layer of padding to fill out the areas that were too flat. It was rather dismaying that, despite Victoria's being six years older, her sixteen-year-old sister was better endowed than herself in the bosom.

Victoria's thoughts drifted back to her idea for undergarments made of silk. With a few strategic tucks and a bit of quilting to add support, there was a way to make a woman's breasts look bigger. The idea was scandalous, but she couldn't quite let go of it. Surely she wasn't the only woman with less-than-desirable curves.

The more she thought of it, the more she longed to attempt it. If she sewed quickly, she could send one corset to be sold along with the gown she'd made earlier.

But women might not want a corset made of silk, the voice of reason interjected. It might be an utter waste of time. And yet, she couldn't dismiss the idea.

"There. Now look at yourself." Her sister turned her to face the mirror, and Victoria stared at her reflection. It felt foreign, seeing herself dressed like this. The stripes of blue were too pretty, the roses too feminine. In the mirror, she saw a woman with pale skin, and a flush of embarrassment upon her cheeks. Her gray eyes were accentuated by the stripes of blue, and the waistline curved inward before the skirts draped in graceful folds. The gown transformed her into someone else—the woman she was afraid of becoming.

"I should take this off. It fits you better," she started to say.

"You're pretty, Victoria. Don't hide yourself away." Amelia rested her hands upon her shoulders, offering, "Let me do your hair."

Though both of them knew that she'd never attended any sort of ball and never would, Victoria surrendered to Amelia's whims. Her sister ruthlessly twisted and pinned the locks of dark blond hair until all of it rested upon her head in a coronet.

"You look perfect," her sister pronounced, "and when we get to London, we're going to order more gowns for you."

"Amelia, no." Clearly, her sister was ignoring her decision to stay. She helped Victoria with the rest of the buttons while chattering on. "We could visit Madame Benedict's shop."

"I'd rather not." The very idea sent a ripple of dread through Victoria. She'd kept her identity hidden over the past year, sewing ball gowns for Madame Benedict in London. Each of her creations had been unique, but Victoria had resorted to using the services of their neighbor Cain Sinclair to deliver the gowns and bring back the money. He'd also been her source of fabric during the war, and she didn't doubt that Mr. Sinclair had engaged in illegal smuggling to acquire her supplies.

Thus far, her mother hadn't questioned the source of the unexpected funds, for Beatrice had never been good with numbers and didn't understand where the money was coming from. It was a secret Victoria wanted to withhold for as long as possible, for no doubt her mother would be furious. Baron's daughters were not supposed to sew for money.

"Don't you think Madame Benedict will want to meet you?" Amelia continued. "You earned a good deal from the last gowns you sent to her. And you deserve some new clothes of your own."

She ignored the question, for her younger sister didn't understand the need for secrecy. "The gowns I have suit me well enough." She had many that hung untouched in her wardrobe. "I don't need anything, for I'm going nowhere."

Her sister helped her to undress, her mood growing somber. "Victoria, Christmas won't be the same if you're not there."

She braved a smile she didn't feel. "We'll celebrate again when you return. Now, I need to fix this hem."

Amelia cast her a disappointed look. "Do you want me to help you back into your old gown?"

Since it was already dark and they'd finished their dinner, she shook her head. "Help me out of my stays, and I'll get ready for bed."

Her sister obeyed, and Victoria put on a cotton nightgown that fell to her ankles. Then she sat in a rocking chair and picked up her needle and thread. It was easy to fall into the rhythm of sewing, making each stitch neat and even. In time, Amelia left her alone.

Victoria pushed the needle with her thimble, reminding herself that it would be all right. Yes, it would be lonely without her family on Christmas, but she would manage.

She would fill her days with sewing, letting the activity push away her loneliness. And this time, she had a new challenge to attempt. There was still the problem of finding the right fabric, however.

Victoria set aside her sewing and went to open the trunk on the far side of the room. It was filled with old gowns that she and her sisters had played in as children. They had pretended to be grand ladies, hosting parties for their dolls.

She rummaged around the trunk, looking for a bit of silk. Near the bottom, she found a crimson satin shawl that had once belonged to her grandmother. Her mother had loathed the color, believing it was far too garish.

But it was irresistibly soft. She ran her hands over the surface, wondering if it would be too delicate for an undergarment. Frowning, she eyed the door. Downstairs, she heard the sound of her sisters talking, and the low voice of her mother.

There wasn't a great deal of time, but she went to the door and locked it. Then she brought over the stays she'd worn earlier, examining the construction. The boning tended to mash a woman's rib cage, making it hard to breathe. But it was the stiff, unyielding buckram that made it itch.

Victoria stripped off her nightgown until she stood naked in her room. It was cold, and she shivered as she reached for the crimson satin. Gathering it into a length, she molded it against her breasts, experimenting as she lifted them up to create cleavage.

In the mirror, she stared at herself. The soft fabric enveloped her nipples in a sensual way, making the tips erect. The candlelight cast a golden glow over her skin, and the red satin appeared scandalous.

She looked like a courtesan, a woman about to be undressed.

What would it be like to have a man standing before

her? Would he want to caress the satin? Would it allure him, making him desire her as a woman?

Though she'd never touched herself in that way before, Victoria moved her palms over the fabric. Her breasts ached, and a sensual warmth bloomed between her thighs. She knew, from talks with her mother, that within a marriage, a husband would touch his wife intimately. And that she would enjoy sharing his bed.

She let the satin fall away, baring her nudity before the mirror. For as long as she buried herself within the house, no man would ever touch her. No man would ever want her.

The thought made bitter tears spring up in her eyes, for she simply didn't know how to overcome her fear.

If you enjoyed the excerpt, you may purchase
Undone by the Duke at
www.michellewillingham.com/book/undone-by-the-duke/.
It is available in print, e-book, and audio.

Kindle bestselling author and Rita® Award finalist **Michelle Willingham** has published more than thirty romance novels and novellas. Currently, she lives in southeastern Virginia with her husband and children, and is working on more historical romance books in a variety of settings, such as medieval and Viking-era Ireland, medieval Scotland, and Victorian and Regency England. When she's not writing, Michelle enjoys baking, playing the piano, and avoiding exercise at all costs. Her books have been translated into languages around the world. Visit her website at *www.michellewillingham.com* to find English and foreign translations.

21500690R00151

Made in the USA
Middletown, DE
02 July 2015